THE TREASURE HUNTRESS

BOOK TWO: THE TOMB OF SOULS

BY

RYAN MULLANEY

Cover artwork by Paramita Bhattacharjee

Edited by Margaret Dean

Author's note:

This is the second book in the Treasure Huntress series. It is strongly recommended that you read the first book in the series, *The Serpent's Fang*, if you have not done so already. The Treasure Huntress is an ongoing, long-form story, and not a series of stand-alone novels. Important story points and developments from the first book will be spoiled in this episode.

To get the most out of the Treasure Huntress series, please begin with Book One: *The Serpent's Fang*.

sunbirdbooks.org

1.

Skarstind Mountain, Norway

Simone listened through the howl of night winds but she did not hear the wolf.

She had made camp on a narrow ledge that gave shelter from three sides. Sharp winds raced among the mountainsides, whistling loud and fierce. There was no chance of building a fire that night. The higher she climbed, the more the cold breath of the mountain became an adversary.

The tent gave little shelter from the freezing temperature. She'd pitched it, anchored it heavily, and zipped herself into a sub-zero sleeping bag, curling up into a tight ball to retain as much body heat as possible. She pulled a balaclava over her face and wrapped a scarf around her neck. Only her eyes were exposed. She turned, burying her face sideways into a pillow that was as cold and hard as the mountain rocks upon which she had climbed.

For two days, the wolf had been on her tail. It kept back, either from fear or strategy, as if waiting for an opportune moment. It was unusual for wolves to hunt humans, and equally as unusual for a wolf to travel away from its pack. They depended on numbers when hunting to overcome their prey, attacking from multiple angles to bring down larger foes.

This solitary grey predator had chosen Simone as its target for reasons she couldn't work out. But upon climbing onto the ledge where she made camp, Simone lost sight of the wolf. For all she knew, it had retreated to rejoin its pack.

Simone shivered in the restricted space of the mummy bag. She tucked her feet under her backpack, hoping to give them some extra protection from the elements.

The previous night had been a sleepless one. The wolf stalked a perimeter around her camp, waiting, watching with eyes that glowed in yellow orbs of campfire light. Its paws crunched into the snow, the sound lasting well into the night. After long intervals of circling, the wolf would halt and settle down into the snow, presumably for a rest, Simone thought.

She would, in the darkness. She could hear the panting, the hot breath of the wolf striking the cold snow. She had curled up as still as possible, yet even the slightest movement rang like gunfire.

In the blessed moments where she was able to close her eyes, the vision that greeted her on the other side of sleep would startle her awake after a few short minutes. Every time. Without fail.

Her head would jerk away from the pillow, limbs thrashing inside the zippered sleeping bag. She couldn't get free, forgetting where she was or why she was there. Momentarily, she would come back to the present, grounding herself, understanding that she wasn't in Mexico anymore. She was in Norway, far away from the deeds she had committed south of the border.

Every time her eyelids slipped closed, she saw the blood streaming from the gash in Heather Severn's neck, or the gunshot wound she had inflicted in the stomach of a mercenary whose name she never knew.

The bodies weighed heavily on Simone's mind. She had thought distracting herself would help her forget what she had done. She figured she should do something for herself, busy herself with a task important enough to drive away all the negativity that flooded in when she let her guard down.

Ironically, it was the wolf that provided the distraction. Her fight-or-flight mechanism kicked in, survival instincts overriding all other synapses and processes in her brain. The most basic, reptilian instinct of self-preservation became the norm on her mountain climb. Tonight, the wolf was absent. Simone kept a keen ear toward the wind, listening for the now-familiar sound of paws crunching through snow and panting breath steaming in the frostbitten air.

An hour passed before Simone realized she was finally alone.

She tried for sleep but it eluded her. Twenty more minutes passed and then she turned over, taking pressure off her right side. Her injuries from her expedition to Mexico had healed well, yet a lingering discomfort persisted, exacerbated by the extreme cold. It didn't seem to bother her while in motion, during the physical act of climbing, finding footing and leverage, pulling herself along, pushing herself upward, powering along through ankle-deep drifts. Only when she allowed herself to rest did the memories of the past return to haunt her.

A year prior, she would have laughed at the absurd notion that she might be carrying with her a supernatural curse. The Simone Cassidy of the present didn't know what to believe anymore. She had seen things with her own eyes that she still did not believe. Mystical forces, powers beyond the known realm, magic or voodoo or whatever, she couldn't possibly know for sure what they were. The Aztec dagger she'd found in Mexico had turned her beliefs upside-down. Now it seemed that anything was possible.

On this night, Simone did not laugh at the idea of being cursed. Instead, it scared her.

Simone huddled closer, tightening herself into an even smaller ball, hugging her limbs to her body as she shivered. She was cursed, there was no doubt in her mind. She had once joked with Lincoln Lewis about not sleeping. As a frequent sufferer of insomnia, she was half-right. There were many nights she could not fall asleep. But now, she literally did not sleep. Not since she began her trek up the Scandinavian mountain.

She had rented a small apartment in a little village outside Lillehammer called Svingvoll. The night before she left for Skarstind, she found herself still roaming the apartment past three in the morning.

Desperate for rest, she smoked two joints and downed three or four painkillers - she didn't bother counting. She'd been prescribed a ton after leaving the hospital in California for dealing with her multiple injuries, and nobody - doctor or pharmacist - seemed to care how many she took. They'd sign off on a refill with barely a question asked.

Simone had passed out that morning as the sun peeked above the horizon. Eighty minutes later, she awoke in a cold sweat and finished packing.

At present, the night winds swirled and tossed a light snow disarray. Simone lay awake, listening for the predatory wolf. At dawn, she rose, packed up the tent in an eerie silence, and continued her climb.

She preferred to pack light and carry with her only the bare necessities. It made for quicker travel over uneven and dangerous terrain. Yet even so, in the cold of the mountain's elevation, Simone found herself stopping to unzip her parka and throw off her hood.

Pausing for a breath and a chance to cool down, she pulled from her pack the small journal Clark Bannicheck had given her - the journal her parents had kept. She thumbed through the pages with the limited dexterity of gloved hands, and stopped on a bookmarked page.

Figuring out how to tackle the wealth of information within the travel journal proved a tall order. Most of the writing was her father's, and his handwriting could not have been worse. Simone could make out most of it, but it was her mother's script that paved the easiest way forward.

Simone found a few names in the journal. One of those names was Harald. No surname had been given. The best guess as to his whereabouts was somewhere on the Skarstind mountain in Norway. But there was no date in the book to accompany the name and information. No way to know for sure exactly how long ago it had been written. Harald could have moved far away over the years, or have died of old age.

Her intel was limited, but Simone knew the best way of learning about her past, about the family she never had, was to follow the clues in the journal.

So here she stood, somewhere on the Scandinavian mountain, following the paths until she either found Harald or went back to her apartment to figure out where to go next.

Hood removed, Simone pulled a wool cap over her head and zipped her parka up halfway. A compromise. She had to retain some body heat.

She threw a glance behind her, expecting to see the grey wolf following closely behind as it had been before, but the wolf was nowhere in sight. It had abandoned her.

Simone turned back to the path and continued on.

She entered a stand of thick trees with deep brown bark and snow-covered tops that shut out most of the early day's sunlight. It was as if she was entering a new nightfall, speckled with random hints of daylight peeking in from just above the horizon.

The path, snow-packed and nondescript, was not easy to follow. Simone had to pay close attention to her footfalls, to the winding bends that snaked around a forest floor that snaked in wild, rolling hills and steep drops.

She trudged through the frozen mud. Her progress grew slow. She fought the urge to peek behind to see if the wolf had caught up. She wouldn't be able to hear its approach with all the sound she was making herself. She just had to press on and be ready if any threats closed in.

Simone came to a short cliff wall standing double her height. She looked about, but found the path ended where she stood facing the rock. She must have taken a wrong turn somewhere along the way. Why would the path just end?

There was nowhere else to go but up. Simone found the idea of doubling back and hoping for a different path to be less than desirable. She had to go forward.

Simone climbed, finding her best footing, making sure her handholds were firm. She had climbing gear in her pack, but she didn't think she'd need it to scale this short wall.

Up she went, throwing her hands over the top and pulling herself up the rest of the way. She got to her feet and paused to survey the area.

Ahead, chimney smoke.

The sight was unmistakable. Another cluster of trees lay below, and from within rose the grey smoke of burning wood, steady and complacent.

With renewed vigor, Simone started down the slope that led into the trees.

The passage was narrow, and for a while Simone wasn't sure she had taken the right direction toward the source of the smoke. She stepped out from the cover of trees and came to a sudden clearing, wide and circular. There she found the cabin.

Nestled near a cliffside view of the mountain below, it appeared to have been built by hand, small and rustic. Chopped wood stood in piles as high as the sloping roof. She saw no vehicle nearby in which to travel. It was as if someone had dropped the cabin onto the mountainside from above.

With her heart in her throat, Simone stepped onto the small porch. She swung her pack from her shoulders - a blessed break from bearing the weight. Pulling off her gloves, and knocked on the door.

Simone listened. She could hear the crackling of a fire beyond the door. Someone had to be there.

But nobody came to answer.

Simone knocked again. The door was jerked open before her hand could strike the wood to finish the knock.

Startled, she jumped away from the man that stood before her, one hand on the door and another holding a rifle at his side. A long white beard covered most of his leathery face. He wore only long undergarments, stained and torn. Hunched where he stood, his hard look softened as his eyes fixed on Simone's face, as if he was trying to figure something out in his head.

Simone didn't say a word. She didn't move a muscle for fear of hearing the rifle crack in the cold mountain air. She just stood in the rush of warm air that escaped the cabin's open door, waiting.

The old man set the rifle against the inner wall and raised a slow, unsteady hand to Simone's face. She stepped away before he could reach her.

"You have your mother's eyes," the old Scandinavian man said.

Simone froze in place. "Harald?"

His face lit up at the sound of his name. A toothless smile broke through his untamed beard. "Come inside, child. Please, come."

He stepped aside, holding the door open for Simone to enter. Cautiously, she stepped over the threshold.

Harald closed the door and instantly the cabin was as hot as a summer day.

"I have soup in the kettle," he said. "I will fix you a bowl. You must be chilled from your journey."

Harald busied himself in the corner of the cabin that acted as the kitchen. Simone lingered near the door for a quick exit should this man turn out to be someone other than a friend of her parents. She hoped her mother and father wouldn't write down the names of their enemies in their journal. If that was the case, Simone might have just walked into her death.

Simone removed her parka and hat, holding on to them. There wasn't anywhere nearby to lay them down or hang them up.

"You may throw your things on the chair near the fire," Harald called without looking back.

Simone hung her parka over the back of the chair near the fire and stuffed her hat in one of the pockets. She elected not to sit.

The cabin was every bit as small on the inside as it looked from the outside. Everything was made from wood gathered from the surrounding forest. An assortment of trophy heads adorned the walls.

The only source of food out in the wild, Simone thought.

She found nothing modern. The cabin had no electricity, no running water, no internet. This man had totally cut himself off from the outside world. She assumed he didn't have a cell phone considering there was no place to charge it. She had left her own phone at the apartment, knowing there was small likelihood of service up on the mountain.

Gazing around, Simone felt strangely at home.

"Please, sit." Harald brought a steaming bowl of soup to the table at the center of the room. He turned the chair away from the fire so Simone could sit and eat at the squat little table.

"Thanks," she said, and eased herself into the chair. "You're not eating?" She noticed he did not have a bowl for himself.

"I already have, child." Harald pulled a rocking chair from the corner and rested his old bones, rocking gently as he watched Simone pick up the spoon.

She held the utensil, not at all ready to dig in no matter how loudly her stomach growled. It smelled delicious, but … who was this guy, really? She weighed the odds of the soup being poisoned.

"You knew my mother?" Simone asked instead of eating.

"Citra, yes," Harald said, nodding with a sense of fond remembrance. "I can see her life in you, child. You are one and the same. There is no doubt in my mind that you are her daughter, are you not?"

"Yes," Simone said.

"I knew your father, as well," Harald continued. "A strong man in body and mind. Full of drive." A moment of somber reflection gave the old man pause.

Simone watched, spoon clutched in her hand, waiting to hear more, her meal an afterthought.

Harald cleared his throat. "I regret not being able to meet you sooner. I received word of your mother's pregnancy late. I wished to be in America to welcome you into the world, child, so I hope that my welcoming you into my home can make up for it in some small way."

Simone swallowed the emotion that had risen in the form of a lump in her throat. "It does," she said. "My name is Simone." She wasn't sure he knew what her name was.

Harald leaned back in his rocker, hands crossed over his belly. "Simone," he said with a smile, listening to the sound of the word. "A beautiful name."

"How do ... how did you know my parents?" Simone asked.

Harald grinned. "You made the journey up the mountainside and found me on your own. That was the first indication you were a Cassidy child. Your parents were also quite skilled in locating things that wished not to be found. I aided them on several occasions when they found themselves in the Nordic lands."

Simone looked down at the soup bowl. She lowered the spoon into the steaming broth, raised it to her lips, and tasted it.

"Do not burn yourself, child. Let it cool."

"It's very good," Simone said. "Thank you."

"Now, I must be the one to ask some questions of you," he said. "For years, I wasn't sure you were even alive anymore. After the accident, I heard nothing. I assumed you, also, had passed. My heart fills with joy to know that was not the case."

Simone looked at her soup once more, unsure of what to say. The emotions that flooded through her just then had no name.

"It appears, to my old eyes, that you have followed in the path of your mother and father," Harald said. "How long have you known?"

"Known what?"

"What you know now."

Simone thought about how to respond. How much to give away? How much did Harald already know?

"I only just learned about them," she said carefully. "It was very recent. I saw your name in their journal and that's how I - "

"Their journal?" Harald stopped rocking.

Simone hesitated. "Yes."

A long moment passed before Harald leaned back in the rocker. "So, you have met Clark Bannicheck."

Simone rested the spoon in the soup bowl. "Yes. Is that good or bad?"An expression of deep thought crossed the old man's weathered features. "You have worked with him, yes?"

"I have." She decided she wasn't going to tell him about Mexico. If he didn't already know, he didn't have to.

"Hmm." Harald fell again into a state of contemplation.

Simone wanted to finish the vegetable soup but it felt as if any movement would break the old man's trance. She couldn't eat any more until she heard everything he had to tell her.

Harald exhaled a deep breath. "I must say, child, that when you leave this cabin , when you find your way down the mountain and return to the place you call home, I say … proceed with great caution."

"Caution?"

"These people you work with - "

"I don't work with them," Simone interjected. "It was a one-time thing."

"Nevertheless, Harald continued, "these people, they are not who they say."

The blood ran cold in Simone's veins. "What do you mean?"

"If you choose to work with them again, do so with great care."

Simone felt her heart rate rising. "I don't understand. Who is Clark then, really?" There was something he wasn't telling her.

Harald opened his mouth to speak, but chose not to say what was on the tip of his tongue. Instead, he said, "Clark is not always forthcoming."

"He isn't the only one," Simone said, the implication obvious.

She didn't know what Harald was keeping from her, or why it couldn't be said, but her thoughts fell on the journal - which had been given to her by Clark.

"Did he…" She found the words hard to say. "Did he do something … to my parents?"

Closing his eyes, Harald shook his head gently. He then looked to Simone. "Clark is not that malicious. He, too, was a friend of your mother and father. They had disagreements - moral disagreements - but they always found a compromise."

Simone understood the flexible morals of Clark, who had sent her into a far greater danger than she was told. The secrecy surrounding what happened to one of the most powerful objects Simone had ever seen or heard of - the Serpent's Fang - never sat well with her. Were they going to bury it so its powers could never be wielded again? Sell it for a fortune beyond imagination? Or use it as a weapon in combat?

Simone hated the fact that she might have been used for such a nefarious end.

"Tell me more about them. My parents."

She didn't wish to dwell on the negative for too long. She'd rather hear about her family, hoping to learn more about herself in the process.

There were few people in the world who could tell her what she wanted to know. One was Clark Bannicheck, a man she didn't necessarily trust to be open with her. Another was the old man sitting right in front of her, opening his home to her in spite of his wish for seclusion.

Harald pushed himself up from the rocking chair with an effort. Simone rose to help but he waved her away.

"Please, sit." He took the soup bowl. "I will get you more to eat. We have plenty to discuss. I hope you are not on a tight schedule."

Simone sat down in the chair, watching Harald move toward the kitchen area. "No," she said. "I don't have anywhere to be. Just here."

* * *

Simone stepped onto the porch and pulled her hat over her head. Taking her pack from where she left it on her way in, she hoisted it onto her shoulders and turned back to Harald. "Thank you. For everything."

"You are always welcome here, child. I may not be the easiest man to reach, but that does not mean I do not wish to speak with you again." He held out a bony hand for her to shake.

Simone bypassed the handshake and went in for a hug. Her gratitude for the old man's hospitality could not be measured. She felt a pang of sadness that she couldn't do anything for this man that would equal what he had done for her.

"I would love that, too," she said with emotion rising in her voice. She turned to the majestic view of the mountain pass that could be seen from the porch. "It's really beautiful here."

"Be safe on your journey," Harald said.

Simone nodded and smiled. She stepped off the porch.

"And Simone…"

She stopped to look back.

"Remember. If Clark should contact you again, proceed with caution."

"I will." Simone took a breath to prepare herself for the long trek back down the mountain. "Thank you, Harald. I'll see you again. I promise."

"I look forward to the day." The old man smiled warmly and waved as Simone departed.

She walked toward the path that had led her through the thick trees. She expected to make a good distance back before having to set up camp for the night.

Before Simone stepped into the forest, a great howl resounded from the mountain pass. The trees grew silent, and a light snow fell.

She froze in her tracks, breath steaming in the air. She turned her ear toward the sound of a wolf waiting for her somewhere down below.

2.

Svingvoll, Norway

She'd been living in the little village near Lillehammer for two months. Not counting the days it took to climb up and down the mountain, she had not missed a workout.

After another sleepless night, Simone got up at the first inkling of dawn as the black of the night melted into the beginnings of an indigo-hued March morning. Every morning, she would ride her bicycle 31.5 kilometers from her apartment in Svingvoll to a gym in Lillehammer, spend two hours on whatever strength-training regimen she had mapped out for the day, grab a protein shake, and ride the whole way back.

On this particular sun-filled day, Simone rode with a determination that blocked all thoughts from her mind. It was a meditative practice, to push herself as hard as she could, to reach new limits and arrive back at the apartment feeling as though her time had been well spent.

She pedaled around a street corner and down a little slope before swinging around another turn and coming to her building. Hitting the brakes hard and skidding to a sudden stop, Simone nearly fell from the bike when she saw him sitting on the front steps.

"Lincoln…"

She couldn't think of anything to say. The two hadn't seen each other since they met for drinks following her recovery in California. April had been there, too, to say goodbye before they started on new legs of their individual journeys.

"I hope I'm not intruding," Lincoln said, hands tucked in the pockets of his winter coat.

Simone locked the bike to the rack near the street and stopped to catch her breath from the effort of riding hard after a long workout.

"Why are you here?" she asked.

"It's good to see you, too."

She saw a subtle flinch of hurt cross his face. "I'm sorry," she said. "I don't like surprises."

"I figured you would have seen this coming. We've called, left messages…"

"And I figured you might get the hint." Simone passed him as she went toward the door. "I'm not interested in another mission."

Harald's words returned to her - Clark could not be trusted. She should proceed with caution. A cryptic statement that Simone couldn't make heads or tails of, but it had her instincts telling her the warning might also apply to the other members of the group, as well - Lincoln and April, specifically.

Simone unlocked the door, pushed it halfway open. She turned to Lincoln. Against her better judgment, she said, "Want to come in?"

She held the door open and Lincoln stepped inside.

"Make yourself at home." Simone went straight for the fridge and drank a fruit smoothie she had prepared before she left for the gym.

Lincoln eased toward the center of the small living space, curiously devoid of any furniture apart from an air mattress, a tiny nightstand, and one proper chair.

"I could say the same to you," he said jokingly. "You did get paid for the - "

"Yes," she said, cutting him off, not wishing to hear any references to their past endeavor. Of that, she said no more.

"What do you do now?" he asked.

"For money?"

Lincoln nodded.

"Avoid needing it."

"Fair enough," he said.

Simone finished the smoothie and set the glass in the sink. "Do you want anything?"

"Just to talk."

"About what?" Simone sat on the air mattress cross-legged. "And I'm sorry if I smell. It was a long ride."

"That's actually why I came here," Lincoln said. "I could smell you from the States. People are starting to complain."

Simone suppressed a smile as best she could. She was never very good at that. "Do you do stand-up in your spare time? That was really good."

"As a matter of fact, I just quit the whole treasure hunting thing to pursue my comedic talents full-time."

"Pursue your comedic talents? I don't think anyone can help you find those." One second later, Simone burst into laughter.

"Funny," Lincoln said with a grin. "Actually, I came to talk about finding something much different."

Simone's laughter settled gradually as she found herself waiting for a proposition she wasn't sure she wanted to hear.

"I really wish you hadn't come all this way, Lincoln."

"You haven't even heard what I have to say. Have you quit?"

"Quit what?"

"I haven't seen your name mentioned anywhere since we got back from Mexico. You made quite a name for yourself before then."

"I've been busy," Simone said with her eyes cast down to her feet. "I have a personal project I'm working on."

"Your parents?" Lincoln asked.

Simone raised her eyes to meet his. After a moment, she nodded.

Lincoln rested his elbows on his knees and propped his chin on his threaded fingers. Neither of them said a word for an interval as neither party knew how to properly continue the conversation.

"I'm going to get cleaned up," Simone said. "Then we can talk about whatever the new thing is." She stood. "But on one condition."

"Name it."

"We do it over drinks. For tradition's sake."

Lincoln's brow narrowed. "Simone. It's still morning."

Simone shrugged. "It's almost noon."

Lincoln smiled and sat back in the chair, taking note of the lack of anywhere else to sit. "I'll wait right here, I guess."

* * *

In the shower, Simone stood under the spray of warm water, letting it hit her face and massage the top of her head.

Looking down at herself, her eyes traced over the scar near her ribs from Heather Severn's knife. She looked at the marks on her arms from where she cut herself on the barback mirror.

Reminders of the nightmare she had lived through in Mexico.

Going back to work for Clark hadn't been a consideration before Lincoln showed up. Simone preferred to do her own thing, a thing that did not involve being stabbed or shot at.

Or shooting others.

She steadied herself against the shower wall as a wave of painful memories struck like an ocean's tide crashing down and dragging her under the surface.

April was right when she had said they would do what they had to in order to survive when it came to that point, and Simone did not like the person she had become in Mexico. She'd done things she never thought she was capable of doing, had seen the horrors of death, had taken life herself.

These were things she could never un-see.

The nightmares greeted her every night when she settled down and closed her eyes. She found not sleep, but the twisted, terrified face of Heather as she groped at the hole in her neck. She saw the face of the man she had shot. She saw herself jumping off a cliff on a hope and a prayer that she would land safely in the raft.

Who was this person who had seen and done these things?

The hot water ran out and the shower turned bitter cold, yet Simone did not move. She thought only of rest, thinking about how to drive the nightmares away and be at peace again.

Shutting the water off, Simone stepped out of the shower and dried herself with a towel. She had returned from Mexico feeling as though she had no real knowledge of the world. Even though she traveled all over the globe, she had never encountered a power like the Serpent's Fang. She'd thought such a force could only be imaginary.

Then she saw it with her own eyes. It was real. Magic, mysticism, all the things she had thought were nothing more than tall tales meant to frighten away would-be looters and bandits from plundering the wealth of tombs.

If the Serpent's Fang was real, what else was out there? What other forces were at play in ways Simone could only speculate?

She got dressed in clean clothes as her mind raced. She tried some breathing techniques to calm herself. The prospect of treasure hunting always had a knack for kick-starting her adrenaline with a world of possibilities. Now, it wasn't excitement that had her heart racing in her chest. It was fear.

The question of what a man as wealthy and connected as Felix Enderhoff could do with an artifact as powerful as the Serpent's Fang returned to Simone every night when she lay awake. She felt a sense of gratitude that she helped prevent that from happening, but as she stood in front of the bathroom mirror towel-drying her hair, she could only think of what other artifacts were out there waiting to be discovered - not just by Clark's team, but by other wealthy and connected parties as well.

She didn't know what to think or who to trust. Simone had gone up the mountain in search of answers but came down with only more questions.

Sucking in a deep breath, Simone exhaled slowly. She knew there was only one way to find the answers she was looking for.

* * *

"What?" Simone asked as she finished the last bite of her second full plate of lefse, Jarlsberg cheese, fruit jam, and smoked fish. "You work out a lot, you get hungry."

Wide-eyed, Lincoln sat back and took a swig of beer. "I'm impressed."

Simone stacked the empty plates and moved them aside. "So, here we are."

"Indeed."

"Why don't you tell me what brings you halfway around the world? What is it that couldn't wait until I came back to the States?"

"You were going to come back to the States?"

Simone tilted her head, eyes looking up for a clear answer. "Eventually."

Lincoln finished his drink. "Clark wants you back on the team."

"I'm not one of you, Lincoln. I was working *with* you."

"And what are we?"

Simone hesitated as she tried to find the right word. *Killers?* She knew that would sour the mood.

"I'm a treasure hunter, that's all. I find things. I don't do ... everything else it is that you do."

"You don't have to. That's what we're for, April and I." He leaned in. "We need you, Simone. Without Angelo around, we have nobody to guide our way."

"And what happens when I'm not around anymore?"

Lincoln rubbed a hand down his face - a gesture that told Simone he was frustrated.

"You're not going to get killed, if that's what you're worried about."

"I'm not worried about myself," Simone said.

Baffled, Lincoln threw his arm out. "Then who are you worried about, the people trying to kill us?"

Heads turned in their direction. A server came by to see if they needed refills but Lincoln waved them away.

He lowered his voice. "I know this isn't your typical line of work, but it's important work, Simone. We need someone with your skills, your ability to think on your feet, to figure things out and adapt, to keep yourself together even when things get bad. We need *you*. There isn't enough time to find someone else."

"Find someone else for what?"

Lincoln leaned in closer, his eyes checking the surroundings for anyone still paying attention. Nobody was. He looked Simone in the eye. "Have you ever heard of the Fallen Star?"

Simone drank the rest of her beer. "I have no idea what that is."

A curious look came over Lincoln's face. "For real?"

"Yes, for real. Believe it or not, there are things in the world I don't know about."

Lincoln showed Simone a map of Europe on his phone. "What does this look like?"

She noticed a date stamp at the bottom of the photo. "Europe in the year 1346."

Lincoln swiped to another screen. The same map, but now a dark area covered the lower portion of the image.

Simone noticed the date change. "1349. The Black Death."

"That's right," Lincoln said. "And this…"

He swiped to another screen which showed the entirety of Europe that had been afflicted by the Black Death. All except a circular area in the center.

"What's strange about this?" Lincoln asked.

"Poland," said Simone.

"Why?"

Simone shook her head, thinking. "They were off the beaten path. Rural. It likely spread through the more populated regions first. No doubt some of the more isolated folks would be on the lookout for strangers wandering in, I don't know for sure."

Lincoln put his phone back in his pocket. "It could be all of the above. Or it could be none of the above."

Simone cracked a grin. "I'm waiting for the inevitable *or.*"

"Or," he said with exaggerated intrigue. "Or maybe it was some other reason. Some object, perhaps."

Simone leaned back in her seat. She picked up her beer bottle but found it empty. She put it back down.

"What kind of object, Lincoln? The kind like the Serpent's Fang? And where is the Serpent's Fang, anyway?"

"I don't know," he said. "It's not our job to know. It was our job to find it."

"Why did we go through all that trouble? What did we-" She lowered her voice to a whisper. "-*kill* for?"

"So it wouldn't fall into the wrong hands. You saw what it could do. Would you want someone like Felix Enderhoff with that kind of power?"

I don't want someone like Clark Bannicheck to have it, either.

Simone paused for a moment to collect her thoughts. Whatever it was they were after, it had to have some unfathomable significance, some otherworldly ability that separated it from any old artifact. Otherwise, they wouldn't be after it.

Putting two and two together, Simone said, "The Fallen Star somehow saved Poland from the Black Death. You have a lead on it but not the whole puzzle. Just enough pieces to know what it's all about, and you need me to help you find the other missing pieces. Am I hot or cold?"

"You're burning up," Lincoln said.

"I'm quite enjoying the cold, actually. Norway has been good to me. If I'm going to leave, I need some reassurance."

"About what?"

"That what we're doing is going to help people."

"That's between you and Clark," Lincoln said. "I'm just the messenger."

"What guarantee do I have that he'll tell me what I want to know?"

"None."

"What guarantee is there that the Fallen Star even exists?"

"None."

"What guarantee can you give me that we we'll be alone on this expedition? That there isn't anyone else out there on the same trail looking to shoot anyone who stands in their way?"

"None."

Simone laughed. "You should stick to comedy because you'll never make it in sales."

"Does that mean you're not coming with me back to the States?"

Simone looked to Lincoln and nodded. "It means I am not going back with you."

"Simone-"

"It means I have some business to take care of before I make a decision. You can tell Clark I'm considering the proposal."

Lincoln smiled, with a satisfied nod. "That's how I know you're a good fit for our team."

"Why's that?" Simone asked with intrigue in her voice.

"You're stubborn. We need that quality. There are no dead ends with you, Simone. You either go around them, go over, or go straight through."

"I'll consider that a compliment."

Lincoln stood. He took some money from his wallet.

"I got this," Simone said.

Lincoln waved her comment off. "I got it. For tradition's sake." He pulled his coat on. "We're at Andrews Air Force Base in Maryland. April is already in the field. The longer we delay, the more trouble she can get herself into."

"Understood," Simone said.

"Take care, Simone. It was nice to see you again," he said and turned for the door.

"Likewise. You take care of yourself, too."

He nodded with a smile.

She listened to the clanging of bells as Lincoln pushed the door open and exited. The bells fell silent and Simone found herself alone.

Her heart felt heavy in her chest. She didn't want to go back to working with Clark - and that was before Harald told her to proceed with caution.

Maybe this time it will be different, she told herself. Felix was dead. Heather was dead, and she was allegedly the leader of the SWANN organization Felix had hired, so they would be in disarray, at least temporarily before a new leader stepped into place.

The sooner Simone agreed to the job, the sooner they could get to April and ensure her safety. They could jump on the leads before any other parties knew what the Fallen Star even was. If she acted quickly enough, perhaps they could avoid the dangers they'd found in Mexico.

There was nothing more for Simone in Norway, she realized. She'd found Harald, who had told her everything she needed to know. Now it was on to the next leg of the journey of digging into her parents' past. She didn't even know where that was. She'd have to study the journal and decipher where to go next.

Simone left some money on the table even though Lincoln had already paid for everything. She didn't like people paying her way. According to Harald, she was as stubborn as her father, not wishing to rely on anyone else.

Standing, Simone wriggled her arms through her coat sleeves and pulled her hat on. She had bought herself some bargaining time with Clark by sending Lincoln ahead. She had all the bargaining power, in fact. If Clark didn't tell her what she wanted to know, she wouldn't go. Simple as that.

Simone left the little restaurant and started walking back to her apartment, thinking of the possibility that Clark would refuse to tell her about what she risked her life for in Mexico.

It would be a dead end.

Simone didn't like dead ends. To avoid that possibility, she'd have to do some reconnaissance of her own before journeying to Maryland.

3.

The American Museum of Natural History, New York City, USA

"Simone! Is that really you?"

Georgia Gates ran up to Simone as fast as she could move in three-inch heels and a tight dress. She stood nearly six feet tall when barefoot, and her big hairstyle only added to her imposing stature.

Simone stepped up, arms spread as wide as the smile she couldn't hide if she tried. "In the flesh."

The two old friends embraced in the lobby of New York's museum of natural wonders. Georgia pushed Simone away and held her by the shoulders.

"What took you so long? It's been forever!"

"I know, I'm sorry," Simone said. "I've been busy sorting things out. Never mind that. How are you? How's the family?"

"Kids are growing up too damn fast. Otherwise, things are swell. Can't complain." She ushered Simone along. "Walk with me. Speak. Tell me why you're here. I know you didn't just stop by to chat. That ain't like you, Simone."

"I wish I could," Simone said as they walked. "Just chat, I mean. I started working for this new company."

She took note of the number of museum patrons - too many for her liking.

"Is there somewhere we can talk? In private?"

* * *

Georgia locked the door to her office and indicated a chair for Simone to sit.

"Thanks," Simone said.

Georgia leaned against her desk. "I sit down all damn day sometimes. Other days, I'm on my feet dawn to dusk."

"Sounds like you're keeping busy."

"Yeah, and no thanks to you. You're going all around the world and you haven't brought me back anything since Cambodia. What do they have you doing out there, girl?"

Simone picked at her fingers, unsure of how to broach the subject. "Sometimes, I don't even know." She looked up to Georgia. "But I do have a lead."

"Well, don't keep me waiting. Lay it on me."

"Maybe you already know about it. The Serpent's Fang?"

Georgia shook her head. "What's that supposed to be?"

Simone considered Georgia's answer before replying. "I thought you might have heard something about it recently. Nobody came to you with anything on it?"

"Not until you walked in," Georgia said.

"Hmm," Simone said to herself, her gaze off somewhere in space. "That's interesting."

"What is?"

Simone turned to the door. "Can anyone hear us? How thick are these walls?" Her eyes went up to the ceiling looking for a vent.

"Simone, level with me. You're freaking me out a bit, okay?"

"Okay, I'm sorry. But I found it."

"Found what? The snake tooth?"

"It's not a tooth," Simone said. "It's an Aztec dagger, used in ritual sacrifice."

Georgia grimaced. "Damn."

"It's a dagger, but it's…" She didn't even know how to describe it. "It's something else."

Georgia shrugged, confused.

"Do you know the name Bannicheck?" Simone asked, her voice at a conspiratorial volume. "Clark Bannicheck?"

"I don't know any Clarks or any Bannichecks." Georgia pushed herself away from the desk and paced about. "Should I?"

Simone thought about whether it would be good or bad if she did. "If you do hear that name, I want you to get a hold of me as soon as you can."

"Simone, tell me what's going on. Are you in trouble or something?"

Simone took a breath. It hurt to see her friend so concerned, but she couldn't know everything until Simone knew more herself.

"I'm not in trouble," Simone said. "I'm just…I don't know … confused or something. Can I ask a favor?"

"Anything. You know that."

"Keep an ear open for any word on the Serpent's Fang, or the name Clark Bannicheck. But don't go looking for anything - and definitely not on a work computer. It's probably not a big deal, but I'd rather be safe for now."

Georgia leaned against her desk once again. "You said you found it already?"

Simone gave a nod. "In Mexico. It's … pretty remarkable. If you don't hear about it, that will tell me everything I need to know."

"What do you need to know?"

"Where it is now."

Georgia let this idea simmer for a moment. "And you gave it to this Bannicheck guy."

"I did," Simone said with reluctance flavoring her words. "This company, I think they're affiliated with the military somehow."

"What are they called?"

"I don't even know. We met on an Air Force base. They had me do some tests, like physicals and stuff, I guess to make sure I was healthy enough."

Georgia laughed out loud. "You? Healthy enough? Simone Cassidy? They know you almost went to the Olympics, right?"

"Yeah, almost," Simone said.

Georgia, Simone's college roommate, had taken Simone's place on the USA athletic team after Simone had tested positive for marijuana following the World Championships. Georgia came home with a bronze medal in the heptathlon - Simone's preferred event.

"Anyway," Simone continued, "When I got back, they had me sign a ton of paperwork, like two hundred pages or some crazy amount. It was a mountain of paperwork. Non-disclosure and everything - which I'm violating by telling you this."

Georgia sighed. "You never were the best at following the rules."

Simone shrugged with a grin. It was true - she liked to make her own way. Sometimes that meant harmlessly disobeying a few laws. Hopping fences to explore abandoned factories - an adolescent pastime which she credited with jump-starting her love of exploring. Other times, it meant missing out on her Olympic dream because she made the wrong choice at the wrong time. She didn't have many regrets in life, but that was one of them.

"All right," Georgia said. "I keep an ear to the ground in case this Bannicheck guy shows up. What about you? I can pull out the couch if you need a place to crash. How long are you in the city for?"

Simone looked to the wall clock. "About forty more minutes."

"Forty minutes! Girl, you weren't kidding when you said the new gig was keeping you busy. Where do they have you going now?"

"Maryland. Then, I don't know." Simone stood. "I better get going."

"You better come back," Georgia said, her voice stern. Simone knew she wasn't joking around.

"I'll be in touch. And don't forget - message me as soon as you hear anything."

"You'll know as soon as I do."

Simone leveled a serious look at her friend. "This conversation doesn't leave this room. I mean it. Don't even say the word 'serpent' or the word 'fang'."

"My lips are zipped," Georgia said.

They embraced again. Simone said, "Thank you. And I'll be back. I promise."

* * *

The smell of street food mingling with the stench of the street itself made Simone's stomach turn as she walked down the city sidewalk.

The din of commotion everywhere, the blaring of horns and sirens, the sheer humanity crammed into one little area - Simone didn't understand any of it. She thought about being back up on the Scandinavian mountain huddled in her sleeping bag in total isolation.

A part of her thought Harald had it figured out, sequestering himself away from the rest of the world to live as a hermit, yet another part of her considered that if she ever did have to live in a city again, New York might pair well with her insomnia. It would make for an interesting time, at the least.

As kind as Georgia was to offer her apartment as a couch-surfing opportunity, Simone couldn't accept. She had to keep moving. She had a train to catch, and then a flight to Maryland.

A desire to know the truth about Clark and his team had her moving with the hungry momentum of a shark, constantly looking to feed, never stopping.

Sharks were one of the oldest creatures on the planet, existing even before trees. Whatever primal instinct drove them to be the perfect machine, unchanged for thousands of years, that was the instinct Simone felt in that moment as she pressed through the teeming throng of Manhattan foot traffic.

If Clark was not to be trusted, if he was hiding details of their operation from Simone, then there was the possibility - no, probability - that he wasn't being totally forthcoming about her parents.

Simone boarded the flight to Maryland that day knowing she had leverage on Clark. He needed her skills. If he wouldn't be honest with her, she could simply walk away and he might never find the Fallen Star.

Or she could find it herself, and then she would truly have all the leverage.

* * *

Simone stepped off the plane at Joint Base Andrews in Prince George's County, Maryland to the cold reception of a single uniformed crewman who took her bags and escorted her directly to the 79th Medical Wing. Not a word was exchanged between them.

Once inside, Simone was instructed by the woman at the reception desk to sign in and told that someone would be with her momentarily.

She sat in a tiny waiting area with bare, beige walls for only a minute before a nurse stepped through an interior door and called the name "Simone?"

Standing, Simone noticed right away that the thirty-something nurse with a blonde ponytail in the doorway was the same young woman from Edwards AFB back in California.

Oh, great.

Faking a smile as best as she could, Simone approached. "We meet again."

Humorlessly, the nurse held the door open. "Down the hall, past the counter. Second door on the right."

Simone located the room and stepped inside, hopping up on the exam table.

The nurse plopped Simone's file down on the table and took a seat with such exasperation, Simone couldn't tell if the young woman was faking or not.

With a deep, steadying breath, the nurse opened the file and examined the newest pages at the top of the stack.

After a silent moment brimming with stress, the nurse swiveled around in her chair and shook her head in confusion at Simone.

"Why?" she asked. "Why do you do this to yourself?"

"The stab wounds?" Simone asked. "Someone else did that."

The nurse snatched a page from the file. "Multiple stab wounds, a cracked rib, contusion on your right quadriceps, lacerations on your arms and hands, extreme blood loss, concussion - thankfully mild."

"Concussion…" Simone thought about when that could have happened. "Must have been when I - " She stopped suddenly, wondering if the nurse knew about her jump off the cliff. "When I fell," Simone said with a nod of faux confirmation.

The nurse returned the page to the file and faced Simone with stern eyes. "I don't even know what to say to you, Simone, but there's going to be a day when you push yourself a little too far, and I'm going to have to give you some bad news. Hopefully it'll be me telling you that you can't go out on any more expeditions, that your body can't handle the physical burden anymore. I hope it won't be me telling you that you may regain some feeling in your limbs but there's no guarantee. At worst, you won't be here for me to tell you anything."

"I understand," Simone said quietly.

She didn't need the lecture, but she knew telling the nurse that would mean a ten minute reaming out about how lucky she was to be alive after all the beatings her body had taken in the past and how she'd have to start taking this line of work seriously if she wanted to be medically cleared for any more explorations.

The nurse looked down at another page in the file. "It says here you've been refilling your painkiller prescription."

Simone adjusted her seat on the exam table. "I have."

"What can you tell me about that?"

"What is there to tell? I take them, they run out, I refill them. You guys haven't said I couldn't."

"Are you taking them medicinally?" Even though the nurse chose to frame the question in a tasteful way, they both knew what she was talking about.

Simone considered her answer carefully, which resulted in a longer pause than she had hoped for. "I would say so."

"Are you experiencing any chronic pain, joint pain, inflammation, anything of the sort?"

Simone shook her head. "Not anymore. At first, yeah. Breathing with a cracked rib is no joke. But I'm over that." She patted the area near the scar on her side. "Good as new."

"But you still refill the prescription?"

Simone admitted with a short nod. "They sometimes help me sleep."

"Simone, if you're having trouble sleeping, we can prescribe you a different- "

"They don't work," Simone said, stopping the nurse before any more time could be wasted on the matter.

The nurse studied Simone, confused. "What do you mean?"

"I mean sleeping pills don't do anything for me. They just make my dreams crazy as hell and I wake up even more- "

She cut herself off, finding it hard to say too much more about the nightmares she'd been having since returning from Mexico.

The nurse's tone softened. "Even more what, Simone?"

"Tired," she lied.

The nurse exhaled with a displeasure that couldn't be hidden. "Simone, we're on the same side. If there's something bothering you- "

"I'm fine," Simone said with a sour tongue.

She didn't want to be short with the nurse, but she wanted even less to talk about her personal life with someone whose name she didn't even know.

The only thing bothering her at this moment was the nurse. That and where the heck Clark was and when she would get to speak to him about whatever he was sending her off to now.

Sensing an opportunity to gather intel covertly, Simone turned a vulnerable look to the nurse. "What if there was someone else I felt more comfortable talking to?"

"Okay," the nurse said in a voice that hinted at a desire to keep the conversation going now that Simone had opened up. "Was there someone in particular you had in mind?"

Simone played up the moment by thinking to herself instead of answering right away. "I don't know. Who else is there to talk to?"

If they had brought the nurse over from Edwards AFB, surely there was other staff that traveled with the rest of the team. It couldn't just be Clark, Lincoln, April, and this nurse.

"Well, we do have a staff psychologist. He's the go-to guy for matters that can be talked out. It isn't my field of expertise, but I can give him a heads-up that you might want to pay him a visit when you get back."

Simone nodded, slowly at first, then more confidently. "That sounds good. Thank you. Is there anyone else?"

"Like I said, Dr. Mabry is the psychologist. We like to keep each department focused on their own tasks. There's enough paperwork as it is without someone taking on a workload outside of their specialized field."

"I see," Simone said, considering what else she could secretly gather from the nurse. "He'll be wherever you are, right?"

"That's right."

"Is he hard to see, typically? I mean, how many people can one psychologist handle at a time?"

"I'll be sure his schedule is cleared for when you return, unless you'd like to see him beforehand for a preliminary consultation?"

"No, that's fine. Are you sure he'll be available? I don't want to bump someone out if they need to, you know, see him."

"I wouldn't worry about that. The most work he does is with the agents in the field, so he should be ready for when you return."

Okay, small workload, Simone thought. Not too many patients meant not too many agents in the field, which in turn meant that apart from herself, Lincoln, and April, there were not too many others involved that did the type of work that she did. A single psychologist could handle ten clients, maybe fifteen. Simone guessed no more than twenty. If most were field agents, she guessed there were between three and eight others employed by … whoever she was working for.

The nurse rose to her feet and closed Simone's file. "Is there anything else you'd like to go over before we get started with the tests?"

Satisfied, Simone shook her head. "No, I think that's all I needed to hear."

* * *

From the medical facility, Simone was escorted to a private plane getting prepped for takeoff. Nobody roamed freely without an escort.

Near the plane, Simone found Lincoln.

"Glad you could make it," he shouted over the commotion on the ground.

Simone watched her escort take her bags to the plane where three others toiled in preparation for the flight. She did not see Clark anywhere.

"Small crew," she said to Lincoln.

"Just like last time." He motioned for Simone to climb the portable stairs to the plane.

Simone boarded and Lincoln followed. Once inside, he shut the door and much of the noise from outside died instantly.

Lincoln sat in one of the plush seats. "April's already in the field, as usual. We'll be briefed in a conference call once we're in the air."

The private plane was much bigger and far nicer than the rust-bucket deathtrap they'd used to go south of the border on the last mission. Simone was thankful for the soft seats and quiet interior as she made herself comfortable.

"Clark?" she asked.

"He's temporarily unavailable."

"What the hell does that mean?"

Lincoln shrugged. "It means we'll be briefed once we're in the air." He pushed a button and reclined his seatback. "He's been wanting to play our cards close to the vest lately so no intel leaks."

"Is that what happened last time?" Simone asked with trepidation.

"We don't know for sure. Whoever Felix was, he had a lot of money, and money means connections. In that situation, anything's possible. This is just a precaution."

"Not knowing where the heck we're going is a precaution? How are we supposed to prepare? What are we even getting into?"

Simone did not like all of this secrecy. She had joined the crew thinking they would be *more* open, not less. Had she known this was the set-up, she would never have got on the plane.

But it wasn't too late to get off.

Simone pushed herself up from the seat and strode for the door.

"Simone?" Lincoln leaned toward her, not sure what she was about to do.

The door opened before Simone even got to it, and the pilot climbed aboard, shutting the door behind him.

Simone could see through one of the little windows that the ground crew was pulling away the mobile staircase.

"Simone, what's wrong?" Lincoln asked from his seat. "We're about to take off."

"Sorry," she said and turned slowly, feeling trapped on board.

Maybe she could try to convince the pilot she wasn't feeling well, that she forgot something of vital importance, but that would cause suspicions to rise, and if Clark was already on-edge enough to not brief her on their destination, there was no telling what could happen to her if she called off her participation at the last moment.

After all, she was the variable on the last mission - the prime suspect of leaking information. She knew the second she stepped off the plane would be like the blaring of klaxons alerting the entire complex to her possible involvement in nearly derailing the last mission, even though that wasn't the case at all.

Simone returned to her seat. "I wanted to grab something from my bag," she lied.

The engine kicked on. There was no getting off now.

"I recommend getting some sleep after the conference call," Lincoln said. "No telling how long we'll be in the air."

Simone's heart sank as the aircraft began to move. "Do you have any of those small liquor bottles on here, by chance?"

"Should be some. Why?"

"I find it hard to sleep on airplanes," she said.

But it wasn't the airplane that bothered her. It was the unknown destination. It was going to work once more for Clark Bannicheck.

As the plane taxied for the runway, Simone buckled herself in and waited for Clark's call.

4.

Svingvoll, Norway

The streets were unusually crowded.

Solomon didn't understand Norwegian customs, but he had apparently arrived during some form of street market, and a majority of the small town had decided to attend.

Scanning through the crowd, he kept his eyes peeled for the first sight of a woman standing five-nine with an athletic build, deep bronze skin, and long, black hair.

Lilly had said Svingvoll was where he'd find her, the woman named Simone, daughter of the late Mr. and Mrs. Cassidy. And Lilly was never wrong. She might be a ditz at times, but when she was gathering information on someone was not one of those times.

Simone had rented an apartment there recently. Unless she was somehow tipped off, or had some other reason to leave the country, she would still be there.

Solomon pressed through the crowd, making his way down the road toward the address Lilly had told him. Beneath his calf-length coat, he wore a dual holster with a gun at both his right and left side. A tactical knife was sheathed by his boot in case of emergency.

He broke off from the main activity and turned down a little street where he found the address he had been looking for.

From outside, he saw no activity. There was no car parked outside, no bike chained up, no sign that anyone was living there at all.

Only when he was satisfied enough with the idea that nobody was inside did Solomon step up to the door and work a lock pick until he was granted entry.

The door creaked open on its hinges as Solomon stood in the threshold. After a moment, he stepped inside, taking note of the empty interior as he shut the door and locked it. All he found in the way of furniture was a single chair near the center of the room, and an air mattress tucked against one wall with a tiny nightstand beside it.

Solomon felt a pang of displeasure rush through him. He'd missed her. She had to have known somehow that he was coming. But how? That was impossible. Nobody knew. Then why was everything gone except for a chair, a table, and an air mattress?

Solomon went into the little kitchen area and opened the fridge. Inside, he found a case of bottled water and nothing else.

He closed the fridge and opened the freezer. Bags of frozen vegetables and other food items were there still.

Solomon huffed, closed the freezer door, and leaned against the counter. He couldn't figure it out. Non-perishables were gone but the frozen goods had been left behind. There was essentially no furniture, yet an air mattress remained inflated. And not a ratty one that a squatter would have. No, this still had a blanket crumpled at the end.

Assuming Simone had tossed the trash out before she left, Solomon found himself proven correct when he opened the lid to the garbage can to find nothing inside, not even a bag.

A simmering anger grew and he had to take a moment to sit down on the only chair and clear his head before he could think more clearly.

Sitting in the chair, Solomon kept his eyes on the front door.

A long time passed before he moved his hand to his pocket to grab his phone and message Lilly. The message was short and to the point:

She's not here.

Without waiting for a reply, he stood up and headed for the exit, but stopped as a consideration tugged at him from within.

He crossed to the air mattress and tore the blanket away. His suspicions were proven incorrect. Nothing was hidden under the blanket.

Dissatisfied, Solomon tossed the blanket and lifted the air mattress to see what might be hidden underneath.

A book.

An old, weathered, battered and beaten book, leather-bound and tucked far enough under the mattress that he knew it had been placed there intentionally.

Solomon flipped through the chaos of pages, many of which were tucked in loose with no binding to secure them. He saw hastily scribbled notes in what appeared to be two sets of handwriting.

Whatever he held, he knew Simone would want it back. It seemed to be the only object in the entire apartment that was not merely functional. It had a purpose beyond making a sparse and modest living.

It was personal.

Solomon tucked the book in his interior coat pocket and gave the room one last glance.

Satisfied, he went out the same way he had come in, being sure to re-lock the front door before strolling back into the street.

He made his way through town, stopping at every eating establishment and pub that he passed, showing the employee at the register a photo of Simone and asking if anyone had seen his wife, that she had disappeared in the area recently and hadn't been seen or heard from since.

The effort to even find a photo of Simone had proved difficult. She kept a low profile in spite of her increasing fame in the archaeological community. Not everyone was a fan. Many true archaeologists believed she lacked the proper education to go exploring ancient sites, yet others came to her defense, pointing out her desire for the preservation of the lost cities, tombs, and treasures she came across.

Solomon knew this from the Current World Archaeology magazine issue in which he had found Simone's photo. It was the most recent image Lilly could scrounge up, apart from the monochrome security video still image in the Mexican library, which would not suffice to present the illusion that she was Solomon's wife. He had hoped for something more recent, but the year-old photograph in the magazine next to her interview regarding the discovery of Mahendraparvata would do well enough.

"I saw her yesterday, as a matter of fact," the short waiter said before scrutinizing the image more closely. "Yes, she was here, over there in that seat."

Solomon turned to where the waiter was pointing. "Are you certain?"

"Yes, sir. Most certain. She…" He hesitated, gauging how Solomon might react to what he was about to say. "She dined with another man."

"Somebody was with her?"

"Yes, an American with very short hair and a strong physique."

Lincoln Lewis, Solomon thought.

He feigned concern, looking at the waiter. "Did you hear what they were discussing? Anything about leaving? Perhaps on a trip together?"

The waiter shook his head. "I heard nothing, but they did not leave together. The man left first. I'm sorry I could not be more helpful."

"You've been a great help," Solomon said. "Thank you. And if you should see her again, please call this number immediately." A card appeared between his fingers.

Taking the card, the short waiter said, "Is she dangerous?"

"No," Solomon said. "But she is in danger."

He left the restaurant to the tone of an incoming message. He stopped walking to look at his phone.

A message from Lilly. A long one. He didn't read the whole thing. Only the most important words and phrases.

Rental … credit card … hiking gear … tent … sleeping bag … Lillehammer.

Slowly, Solomon turned in a circle, his head tilted slightly back, his fierce eyes scanning the surroundings. He halted on the most likely place to bring a tent and sleeping bag on a hike.

The Scandinavian Mountains.

* * *

"Yep," the young woman with hair falling in her face said from behind the counter of the local outdoors shop. She handed the photo back to Solomon.

"You said she rented equipment? A tent, sleeping bag?"

"Yep. Returned it, too."

Solomon's brow narrowed. "Returned?"

"Brought it all back the day before yesterday." The woman rolled a lollipop from one side of her mouth to the other. "Do you want anything?"

Solomon shook his head. "No, I'm fine. Are you sure it was her?"

"The lady in the photo?"

"Yes. She was the one who returned the gear?"

The woman nodded, failing to care about her hair dangling in front of her eyes. "Yep, it was definitely her. She has that look about her, you know?"

"No. I don't," he said, confused.

"You know, some people just have a look. Your woman there has a look. Some people tell me I have a look, but I don't see it. Do you think I have a look?"

Looking to get out of the conversation ASAP, Solomon pocketed the photo and smiled. "Thank you for your help."

Exiting the shop, Solomon thought only of the mountains near Svingvoll. That had to be where she went. But why? What was up there that drove Simone to Norway?

Lilly had found no reports of any recent archaeological findings in the Scandinavian Mountains.

He stopped to consider the pieces.

She had come to Norway, rented an apartment, rented gear to trek into the mountains, came back to return the gear, and then left the country with one of her colleagues from the expedition to Mexico. The apartment looked barren, but as far as Lilly could tell, it was still rented to Simone Cassidy, so there was a likelihood that she was coming back in the near future.

Wherever Simone had gone with Lincoln was for business, Solomon thought. But the trip up the mountain … that was something different. Something more personal.

Convinced his reasoning was sound, Solomon turned around and went back into the outdoors shop to rent the same gear Simone had used a few days prior.

5.

Somewhere over the Atlantic Ocean

The video call came through thirty minutes into their flight.

Clark Bannicheck's face appeared on the laptop that Lincoln had carried on board for this very purpose. His thick crop of grey hair and neatly-trimmed salt-and-pepper beard had not changed from the last time he met with Simone, but the face beneath seemed to have aged five years instead of one.

Simone didn't know if it was the display on the laptop screen giving the man an aged impression, or if the stresses of their line of work were pushing the 65-year-old man to an early 70.

"I apologize for the delay," Clark said, forgoing any introduction and getting straight to business.

Simone stood behind Lincoln's seat, leaning in to see and hear precisely everything there was to see or hear.

"I'm short on time, so here are the essentials," Clark said. "In a few short hours, you'll be landing at the Brno-Tuřany Airport, Czech Republic. From there, you will meet up with April Farren and proceed to the Church of Saint James."

"What's there?" Simone asked. "I thought the Fallen Star was in Poland."

"I see Lincoln filled you in," Clark said with an emotion that Simone couldn't quite place. It fell somewhere between thankfulness and disappointment. She wasn't sure if one of those halves was all in her head, expecting distrust from the man she was told to be wary of.

"The Fallen Star is not in Poland. We've already concluded an investigation there and I'm sad to say it turned out to be a fruitless endeavor. We gathered only one seed of evidence that the Fallen Star still exists, and that little clue points to the Saint James church in Brno. If you're lucky, you'll walk out of there with what could be one of the most important finds of this century."

"More important than the Serpent's Fang?" Simone asked, hoping to steer the conversation in that direction.

Clark sighed almost inaudibly. "I would focus our efforts on the mission in Brno. Keep a low profile. We don't want to attract unwanted attention."

"Threats?" Lincoln asked.

"As of my last conversation with April, you should be alone on this quest." Clark looked away to something off-screen, then returned. "I'm afraid there's a meeting I must attend. We'll stay in emergency contact only. I wish you both the best of luck, and give April my regards."

He finished with a warm smile before the connection ended.

Simone waited for Lincoln to close the laptop before asking, "So, what am I doing here?"

A pocket of turbulence rocked the aircraft. Simone stumbled, nearly falling, and steadied herself just enough to return to her seat.

"Clark feels you're needed on this one."

"Why?"

"Why didn't you ask him?"

"I'm asking you," Simone said. "This sounds pretty straightforward to me. And besides, this isn't a jungle or rain forest where you might need a guide. It's a church. How big can a church be?"

Simone didn't like that the pieces weren't adding up, which only served to fuel the distrust she had of Clark and his whole operation. She wasn't even sure if she should trust what Lincoln had to say.

Lincoln shrugged, seemingly satisfied with their predicament. "This is the job, Simone. You know how it works."

"No, I don't." She sat up sharply, shooting a cold look at Lincoln. "Where is the Serpent's Fang? Can you tell me that?"

"As I've said, it isn't our job to know."

"And that doesn't bother you? You saw what it could do. How do we know it's not being used for … I don't even know. It shouldn't be used at all."

"It's in a safe place," Lincoln said with finality.

"And is that where the Fallen Star is going, too? A safe place?"

Lincoln huffed in mild agitation. "Simone-"

"Don't try to shut me up on this, Lincoln." She spoke with a fire on her tongue. "If you want me on this team, you need to start filling me in on what we're doing, where we're going, who else might be there looking to kill us.

These are things I need to know. This 'safe place' crap is unacceptable. If you want to drop me off in the Czech Republic and leave me there, go right ahead, but I won't help you anymore until I know for sure we're not giving these powerful artifacts to some tyrannical dictator or somebody looking to do anything with them apart from preserving their history. That's why I'm here, and that's the *only* reason I'm here."

Out of breath, Simone fell back in her seat. She felt a pang of regret for the frankness of her words, but the secrecy had to end, and it felt to her like Clark was actively avoiding an interaction with her, knowing she would press him just as hard as she was pressing Lincoln.

The silence that hung between them felt ready to explode at the first sound, the first movement.

Once it was allowed to settle to a less volatile level, Lincoln cleared his throat. "We're on the same side, Simone. We're here to do good."

Simone stared ahead, not buying it. "The first time we met in Saipan, Clark said you have many different employers. Are they all looking to do good? Is the world really that benevolent?"

Lincoln looked away in an admission of guilt. "That was a lie."

Simone set her jaw in lieu of speaking, knowing she would say something she'd immediately regret.

"We work for the U.S. Government," Lincoln continued. "Clark knew you'd send us packing if he admitted we were military."

Simone smiled an unwonted smile as her suspicions were confirmed. She shook her head. "Why?"

"Would you have said yes if he told the truth?" Lincoln asked.

Simone turned the question over in her mind, trying to convince herself that she wouldn't have. She wanted no part of military activity knowing that her mother and father had died on a military base.

She said nothing.

"Simone, this is important work we do, and we need the best people on the job."

"So," she said, "you're just using me?"

Lincoln sat back, frustrated. "It's not like that."

"Then what's it like?" she asked. "You tricked me into going along right from the start and there's only more secrecy now. I don't appreciate that, Lincoln. I really don't."

"Because you had to see for yourself. In Mexico, the Serpent's Fang. You didn't believe me when I told you what it could do, so there's no way you can sit there and tell me you wouldn't have stayed home and written it off as an old folk tale. But knowing what you do now, would you have come to Mexico?"

Simone's silence gave the answer they both knew was true - she would have said yes. It was the only reason she was on the plane at that moment. If the Fallen Star held some magical power to heal the sick or ward off disease, it *had* to be found.

"If you had told us no, April and I would probably both be dead. But this isn't like last time," Lincoln said in a more calm and measured voice. "We know where to go, what we're looking for, and it's not something that can take lives. It can *save* lives, Simone. Think about it."

No matter how much Lincoln tried to convince Simone, she heard Harald's words in her head louder than Lincoln's. Words of caution. Harald had told her that Clark was a duplicitous person, and now she knew he wasn't being dishonest in that regard.

The only thing she could think of was a question: if Clark was willing to lie to her and use her to get these artifacts by any means necessary, even going to such lengths as to put a citizen adventurer with no military training in harm's way, what was he willing to do once he acquired these ancient relics?

But if Lincoln was right, if the Fallen Star really was an object of healing, what harm could be done with it? The true harm would be in *not* recovering it.

Simone didn't know what to think anymore. Every question that was answered presented even more questions. Like the mythical Hydra, one head coming off spawned two more. And if something as crazy as the Serpent's Fang could be real, what did that say about the Hydra? Thinking about it all made her head hurt.

Abruptly, Simone stood and made her way down the aisle.

Lincoln leaned forward in concern. "Simone, where are you going?"

"To find that liquor," she said without looking back.

* * *

The plane touched down in the dark.

Simone was startled awake by Lincoln's tapping on her shoulder.

"Jesus," she said with a deep exhale, not expecting to find herself where she was. She didn't recall falling asleep. "How long was I out?"

"Quite a long time for someone who doesn't sleep. I'm glad you got some rest, though." He extended a hand to help Simone to her feet.

"Thanks," she said as she stood upright. She must not have drunk much since she felt just fine. Even her headache was gone.

They exited the plane and grabbed their luggage. Lincoln started walking purposefully.

"We have an apartment set up a few blocks away," he said. "That's probably where we'll meet up with April."

"Probably," Simone said with emphasis on the uncertainty of his previous statement.

He shrugged. "Hey, you know April."

"Not really," she said. "I know what she's like, but I don't know *her*, if you know what I mean."

"You mean what are her favorite TV shows, what sports teams does she root for, where does she buy her potted plants, that kind of knowing her?"

Simone chuckled to herself. "I can't picture her doing any of those things."

Lincoln looked back as they walked. "She doesn't."

Simone thought it was a joke, but the expression on Lincoln's face told a different story.

"What does she do, then?" she asked.

"Ask her."

All of a sudden, none of it sounded like a joke. "Why do I get the feeling you're setting me up?" she asked him.

"I'm not," he said. "I'm just a terrible middle-man. Besides, her business is her business. It's not my place to spread it around."

"Fair enough." Simone wouldn't want anyone doing the same about her personal affairs.

Lincoln continued, "And if you can pry something out of her, you're better at interrogation than I am."

"What's that supposed to mean?"

Lincoln gave her a look. "It means you know about as much as I do about April's personal life."

As Simone walked, thankful for the wheels on her biggest piece of luggage, a thought came to her. The thought that April didn't do very much outside of her job working with Clark. And as far as Simone could gather, neither did Lincoln.

She silently hoped that she didn't fall into the same trap, but then it hit her - she didn't have much of a life for herself, either. The trap had already ensnared her before she ever met Clark and his team.

Temporarily living in Norway to seek out Harald had been the most settled-down she'd been in a long time. Years, even. Georgia had acted as if they hadn't seen each other in a lifetime.

Damn, Simone thought. *I better get myself together.*

Looking for assurance, she looked to Lincoln. "What about you?"

"What about me?"

"What do you do when we're not, you know, doing this?" She waited, hoping it wasn't nothing. As much as she enjoyed what she did, her routine had regressed into attempts to sleep, working out, and digging into her family's past.

"I keep to myself," Lincoln said.

Simone smirked. "No kidding."

"Truth is," Lincoln added, "I like to stay busy with work. Everything else feels … temporary."

Simone adjusted the bag hanging from her shoulder. She didn't care much for the answer, but it confirmed her suspicions. With this crew, the job was all they had.

She considered to herself if the work had prohibited other areas of life from intruding, or rather if Lincoln and April had been drawn to the field because they didn't have much else going on.

"This is it."

Lincoln stopped on the sidewalk in front of a nondescript building that looked to hold half a dozen apartments.

Simone looked up at the windows, all of which remained dark. The front door opened and April Farren ushered them inside.

"Didn't think I'd see you again," she said as Simone passed by.

"I'm as surprised I'm here as you are," Simone said. "How are things?"

"Things are best discussed in private."

With that, April closed the door and led the party to the third floor apartment they had rented for the occasion.

Lincoln and Simone dropped their gear once inside the room. Simone saw that each window had been blacked out from the inside and all the curtains were drawn, giving the outside impression that nobody was home.

She also noticed that April was already dressed in black pants, boots, and a dark shirt with the sleeves rolled up, her mess of fiery red hair tied back.

"Are we going somewhere already?" Simone asked.

April fixed her with a look that spoke of the obvious. "Why do you think we're here?" Her eyes went to Lincoln. "Did you get a briefing?"

"You could certainly call it brief," he said. "Clark was preoccupied, so you're going to have to fill us in on the finer details."

April let out an exasperated breath. "Okay, long story short, we're going tonight. Grab what you need and let's hit the road." Lincoln looked curious. "Why tonight? What's wrong?"

"Nothing's wrong, but you know how news travels. Besides, the dark will help us. It's too risky going in during the day."

"What's so risky about going into a church in the daytime?" Simone asked, not understanding. *Everyone goes to church during the day. How is that suspicious?*

April double-checked the ammo magazine of her handgun, then jammed it back in and slid the gun in the holster at her belt. "We're not going *in* the church. We're going under it."

Lincoln stopped what he was doing. "Under it?"

"Catacombs," Simone said with faint recollection. "It opened to the public a few years back. I remember reading about it."

April nodded. "There was a priest at the church who claimed to have found a hidden chamber inside the ossuary. When asked about it, he said he it was just a hole in the wall, and that there was nothing special inside. Just more bones. He died less than a year later."

A shiver raced up Simone's spine. Perhaps he too was cursed.

April continued, "But before he died, an altar boy said the priest instructed him to take a box down into the ossuary and place it within the hidden chamber and seal it back up. He didn't ask what it was, but he went ahead and did it. He put it back, but the hole in the wall leading to the chamber was too large for the boy to do anything about it. He's just a kid, so he told the other priests and they're planning to get a crew down there sometime this week. If we don't go tonight, we might not get down there at all."

The trio exchanged a look. Lincoln then turned to April.

"So, how do we get inside?"

6.

Brno Ossuary, Czech Republic

Rain fell steadily on the cobbled streets.

Sparse lighting around St. Jacob's Square, on which the church was located, allowed the group a stealthy approach. The wet night seemed to be keeping most of the town indoors. The trio went unnoticed.

Simone half-expected guards stationed around the perimeter, but the building appeared to her eyes to be just another old European church.

"Around back," April said just loud enough to be heard over the rain. She pressed by the others to lead the way.

Following her lead, they came to a short iron fence and a stairway leading below the house of worship.

"Down there?" Simone asked.

April responded by descending the pitch-black staircase. Lincoln exchanged a look with Simone, shrugged, and followed April downward.

Simone felt her way cautiously down after Lincoln, careful not to slip on the steps in the blackness. Rain dripped endlessly from the rim of her boonie hat. She was thankful she thought to wear it.

They came to a thick metal door at the bottom of the stairs. April fiddled with a lock pick in the padlock that secured the door.

"What are you doing?" Simone asked rhetorically, not assuming the plan was to actually break in like thieves.

"What does it look like?" April kept working at the lock, looking frustrated with herself, as if she had practiced this before but couldn't perform the task as well in the dark and the rain.

Simone tapped the back of her hand against Lincoln's arm. "We're really doing this?"

"Yeah," he said as if it should have been obvious.

"Isn't there another way?"

She didn't like the idea of being a grave robber for hire. There was a distinct difference, in her mind, between climbing through old temples and tombs in the wild, and breaking and entering a private building that still belonged to someone.

And a church, no less. She had never been a religious person, but after seeing what had happened in Mexico, Simone didn't know what to believe anymore.

Suddenly, the idea of respecting higher powers felt like the right thing to do.

Lincoln leaned toward April. "How much longer?"

"Shut up and let - got it."

With a metallic *click*, the shackle opened. April pulled the lock away and gave the door a nudge with her shoulder.

The resulting sound of the heavy door swinging open on old hinges resounded in the tiny stairway like a locomotive. Simone's eyes darted toward the surface, but there was no one around to hear.

"Come on," April said with agitation, her hair drenched from the rain. She hadn't thought to wear a hat.

Simone ducked inside and April eased the door shut behind them. The sealing of the door sounded to Simone like the lid of a stone sarcophagus shutting them in for eternity. A frosty chill had the hair on her arms standing on end.

April clicked on a flashlight. "It should be this way," she said and proceeded deeper into the shadowy catacombs.

Simone followed close behind, wondering exactly why she was brought down beneath the church. April and Lincoln seemed to have everything under control. She didn't need to be here, yet here she was.

Harald's words of caution returned to her. She gave a quick shake of her head, raindrops cascading from the brim of her hat, but the idea stuck - should she trust April and Lincoln?

As they pressed inward, Simone wondered why April needed a gun in the ossuary. She opened her mouth to ask but kept the words to herself. A strange part of her was thankful that one of them was armed in case something did go down.

Before long, the party came to a central hallway. April shone the light on the walls until a light switch was spotted. Simone flipped it and a yellow glow from overhead lighting filled the subterranean cavern.

April clicked the flashlight off. "Here we are."

Simone gazed about, mouth agape at the sheer number of bones piled all around. Skulls on top of skulls, hundreds and hundreds of them piled from musty floor to arched ceiling. Bones covered every inch of every wall, every curve of every bend. Radius, humerus, ulna, femur, tibia. Her head was spinning from the macabre display, spinning too fast to gauge how many dead there had to be down here, but the number, she knew, was staggering.

"Quite a sight," Lincoln said as he swiveled his head around, gazing upward at the skeletal stacks.

Upon closer inspection, Simone realized that it wasn't the overhead lighting that gave the bones their yellowish tint. They were just that color.

"These have been buried down here since the sixteen hundreds," April said. "They never saw sunlight."

Simone swallowed. The whole thing was making her feel uneasy, every part of it.

"We're looking for reddish bones," April said. "Those would be the plague victims, so that's probably where we'll find the Star."

"Probably," Lincoln said with emphasis.

"Shut up and follow me." April started down one of several hallways.

Simone hurried up close to Lincoln so they could speak privately as they walked. "Are you armed, too?"

He looked back, his brow narrowed. "What?"

"I said are you armed," Simone repeated.

Lincoln snorted a laugh. "You're afraid of some old bones? Seriously?"

Simone stepped around a dozen skulls scattered on the floor. "What does she need a gun in here for?"

Lincoln's face scrunched up and he waved the comment aside. "She's always armed. It's mission protocol."

He paused, his eyes scrutinizing Simone, looking not at her, but into her.

"Is your head in the game, Simone?"

Caught off guard by the question, Simone nodded with confidence. "Yeah, my head's in the game."

Lincoln's gaze hung on Simone for a wordless moment. "Okay," he said. "If you see anything, let me know."

"Likewise," she said, and they continued down the narrow passage.

She didn't need to ask what kind of things he was referring to. The message was clear. It was the unbelievable things. The things she assumed couldn't exist. The kind of things that kept her awake at night shivering in a cold sweat.

Simone suddenly understood why April carried a gun in the ossuary. In this particular line of work, nothing was ever guaranteed.

Simone reached for the knife strapped to her thigh. Feeling the cold metal against her fingertips gave her the reassurance she needed as she followed the others into the unknown.

"There," April said as she came to a stop.

The three of them stood in single file, the passageway too narrow for two bodies abreast. Simone peered around Lincoln to see what had captured April's attention.

A chained-off section of the crypt stood before them. Skulls were piled on either side, dozens of them, perhaps a hundred or more.

April clicked the light on again and aimed it at the skulls at her feet. "These must have been stacked up in front." She moved the light up, shining it beyond the chain and into the new hallway.

Simone traced her fingers along the edge of the hallway. Something didn't add up. "I thought you said it was just a hole in the wall," she said to April.

"I did."

"This is quite a perfect hole."

"I haven't been down here this far," April said. "I'm just telling you what I heard."

Lincoln unhooked the chain. "It seems as if your priest may have been hiding more than he let on. Who wants to go first?"

"He died, right? The priest?" Simone asked.

April nodded her head.

"Great." With a deep breath, Simone stepped forward. "I guess I'll go. I'm already cursed." She made it sound like a joke.

"Here." April handed her the flashlight. "Want this, too?"

Simone turned back to see April holding the gun out for Simone to take. "I'd feel better if you held on to it," she said. "You're a better shot."

And willing to pull the trigger.

Simone, on the other hand, wasn't sure if she could ever hold a gun again in her life.

She aimed the flashlight ahead, listening to her footsteps as she moved, hearing April and Lincoln follow close behind. There was no lighting in this section of the ossuary. The only light was the light Simone held in her hand.

Until…

Simone stopped without warning.

"What is it?" Lincoln asked.

Simone stared ahead at the shaft of light - red light - pouring from a room adjacent to the dark hallway. "There's something up ahead, to the left."

April pressed to the front to see what it was. "I'll check it out. Keep looking."

Simone watched as April jogged ahead until she was swallowed whole by the darkness. Seconds later, her silhouette crept into the red-lit room.

Panning the flashlight, Simone found another hallway branching off from where she stood with Lincoln. "This way?"

"Might as well," he said.

They passed through the black, guided by the flashlight's beam.

"Still believe you're cursed?" Lincoln asked.

Simone grinned. "Someone once told me that it's not a matter of belief. It's either real or it's not. I didn't believe him when he said it, but … he was right."

"The difference between then and now," Lincoln said, "is the person who told you that had evidence to back up his claim. He wasn't forced to add two plus two. He looked and he found four."

"You're asking me if I have evidence?"

"Naturally."

Simone huffed, knowing she couldn't produce any physical evidence or point to any real-world manifestation that proved she was, in fact, cursed.

"It's not that simple," she said. "Some things, you just know. That doesn't mean it's not real. It's a feeling, or a sixth sense, I don't know."

"A feeling like what?"

She stopped and turned to face Lincoln. Their eyes met in the dark.

"Like being happy, or sad. Like confusion, not knowing for sure how you feel. It's like being wrong, like you did something you should never have done, and you can't take it back. Like…" She hesitated, turning her eyes away. "Like a nightmare."

Simone forced herself to meet his gaze again, to stare into the gleam of light reflecting in his pupils and gauge his reaction.

He said nothing.

As much as she wanted to convince him of the evidence she saw every time she closed her eyes, to explain just how real it all was to her, that wouldn't do the trick.

Turning back around, Simone held the light before her and continued through the dark. The path bent, forcing Simone and Lincoln around a corner that led to another spill of light from a room on their right.

Simone played the light around on the walls near the room but found no other path to take. They had to enter the room or turn back.

Together, Simone and Lincoln approached the room. They turned the corner in tandem to find a vast circular chamber with skulls covering every wall. Rib cages and spinal cords were arranged across the domed ceiling to form a crosshatched design. It was carefully, meticulously done. Simone didn't know if it was supposed to look as evil as it did.

Lincoln stared with wide eyes. "What in the…"

At the center of the room was an altar, and beside the altar stood the sources of light. Two tall, thin lamps that reminded Simone of some old gothic candelabra. They must have been connected to the main lights in the other areas of the crypt.

"The bones…" Simone aimed the light at the wall of skulls beside Lincoln. "They're red."

Lincoln moved in for a closer look. Indeed, the display in this circular chamber appeared different in hue from the rest of the countless bones in the other areas of the ossuary. These were more reddish than the yellow ones they had seen before.

"Plague victims," Lincoln said.

Simone's head whipped around to the altar, her eyes landing on a small wooden crate, worn and ancient, that rested in the center between the lamps.

She rushed over to it and peered inside, her blood pumping with the rush of discovery.

"What is it?" Lincoln asked, hurrying up to the altar.

Simone stared into the crate with a look of amazement. "It's … gone."

The lid of the crate had already been removed. Simone found it on the floor at her feet. The crate itself contained nothing at all.

"Do you think the altar boy really brought it back here?" she asked Lincoln.

"I don't-"

Two loud *pops* echoed from down the dark hallway. Then a third.

Simone ducked instinctively, her heart rising to her throat. She knew what the sound was. She could never mistake it.

Gunfire.

The circular room fell into sudden darkness as the lights went out.

Scrambling, Simone lifted the flashlight to the room's only entrance.

Neither she nor Lincoln said a word. They listened, waiting for shouts, commotion, a struggle. They heard nothing. No cries of agony, no pleas, no more gunfire.

The Brno Ossuary fell as quiet as the tens of thousands of dead who resided there.

7.

Brno Ossuary, Czech Republic

The loudest sound in the room was Simone's rapid heartbeat.

"I thought you said we were alone," she whispered.

Lincoln didn't look back at her. He held his gaze on the doorway, waiting for any sudden movements.

"Now's a good time to tell me if you're armed," she said.

He shook his head instead of admitting that he wasn't. April had the only gun.

Lincoln abruptly turned his gaze away from the doorway. "If we're lucky, there might be another way out."

Simone hadn't seen one, but it was hard to tell with all the bones covering every wall. There very well could be a secret doorway hidden just out of view, behind a curtain of skulls. That was how this wing of the ossuary had been found, after all.

She reached in her pocket and pulled out a lighter. "Catch."

She threw it to Lincoln who caught it. Simone then clicked the flashlight off and moved toward the doorway.

"Where the hell are you going?" Lincoln shouted in a hushed tone. He flicked the lighter to give the room a tiny amount of illumination.

"Stay here," she said from the shadows. "I have an idea."

The idea was to not get shot, to lurk in the shadows and creep up on whoever was responsible for the gunfire.

April wouldn't shoot unless the reason was good enough. Simone could tell she had significant training and experience just from the way she handled a gun, the way it rested in her hand, the way she aimed, how she held her finger near the trigger. April made a gun look as though it weighed nothing, as if it was an extension of her.

The three shots had been no accident.

Simone shuffled as silently as possible through the black hallway as her eyes attempted to adjust to the darkness. Thankfully, there was only one path for her to take.

The lack of commotion worried Simone as she inched along. April hadn't called out a warning to the others. She was dead silent. Simone considered the fact that she, too, was stuck in a position where she had to be silent and not give away her cover. There were only so many places to hide down here.

The lights going out troubled Simone even more. April wouldn't do that, even as a joke. One thing she knew about April was that she lacked a sense of humor. The girl was all business, all the time. She wouldn't douse their only source of light, and the odds that it failed on its own seemed too low to be real. No, someone had turned them off intentionally.

That meant there was someone else down here.

Simone crept ever closer to the main hallway, clutching the extinguished flashlight in her right hand with her finger sweating on the switch, ready to click it on at a moment's notice.

She listened, to herself and the other sounds in the old crypt. She could faintly make out the steady rainfall hitting the streets and buildings above - but no other noise was heard. Only the faintest shuffle of her boots against the dusty floor. She breathed as shallowly as possible.

Simone rounded the bend. She replayed the journey in her head, retracing the steps in her mind. The entrance to the room April had ducked into should be nearby. A few steps away at most.

A crunch of small stones halted Simone in her tracks. She held her breath, listening.

She wasn't the one who made the noise.

It came from ahead. Her finger rested on the flashlight's switch. There was no further sound.

Just then, another footstep. Simone couldn't see anything. It was too dark for a human to see, even one with good vision like Simone. She listened for the source of the sound. For a reason she couldn't explain, she closed her eyes. It must have been a trick of the mind, but knowing that her vision couldn't work with her eyes shut helped her concentrate on her other senses better, even if it was all in her head.

And then she heard all she needed. The slightest scuff of a footstep lifting off of the old dirty floor told Simone exactly where that person was standing.

She opened her eyes to more darkness, brought the light up, and clicked it on.

Her aim was dead-on as the beam hit the figure directly between the eyes.

He raised his hands to shield himself from the blinding LEDs, and that's when Simone saw the gun.

He reached out with the weapon and fired blindly in defense.

Simone ducked, covering her head and flicking the light off.

The footsteps ran now, hurriedly toward the only exit Simone knew of. She only caught a quick glimpse, but it looked like a man. Even if it wasn't, it didn't look anything like April.

"April!" Simone shouted as the footsteps pounded further away.

She listened for April but heard only a crash of bones spilling to the floor. The sound continued. It seemed to have no end, as if the entire place was going to collapse one skull at a time.

Simone flicked the light on and ran toward the sound.

The overhead lighting flickered back on just then. Simone paused for the briefest moment, then hurried on toward where she thought she had heard the avalanche of bones toppling to the floor.

Rounding a bend, she entered the main chamber where she found April standing near the light switch to the left. To Simone's right, she saw the immense disaster of bones that covered a wide section of floor.

She almost didn't see the body in the center of it all.

Lincoln rushed in behind Simone. "What the hell was that?" he said before catching sight of the mess on the floor.

April strode into the bone pile, doing her best to find solid ground beneath the skulls.

"That was an unwelcome guest."

She began pushing away the bones that covered most of the fourth party.

A cry of anguish sounded from the body. April jerked upright, startled by the sound.

"He's alive." Simone handed the flashlight to Lincoln and darted in to help excavate the injured man.

"Careful, please," the injured man said between strained breaths.

April pulled a mound of bones away, an act which drew another cry from the buried individual.

"Careful, my ass. What are you doing down here? Why did you shoot at me?"

The man gritted his teeth in immense pain. "You took me by surprise. I - *ah!* - I'm here for the same reason you are."

It sounded as if he had a slight accent, perhaps Middle Eastern.

The heavy metal door clanging shut drew all the attention in the room. Lincoln started toward it. "I'll check it out."

He disappeared toward the surface, leaving April and Simone with the unknown man.

"Who are you?" April demanded.

She had her gun holstered. Didn't need it to sound threatening, Simone gathered. April with nothing but her anger would be sufficient.

Gently pulling away some more bones without causing the man any more harm, and without damaging the bones of the deceased, Simone saw the source of the man's anguish.

A long, broken bone protruded from the man's stomach. It wasn't his, but rather something he fell onto in his haste to escape.

"Check him," April said to Simone.

Simone leaned in for a closer look at his wounds. The protrusion appeared to be the only injury he'd sustained.

"I mean *check him*," April said with emphasis.

Simone got the hint. She patted down his pockets. Inside one was a pistol. Hooked to his belt was a knife much like her own, except his was much more ornate, with a carving of an elephant on the metal guard and butt, and fine leather threaded around the tang.

It almost looked like it didn't belong to the man, as he wore simple clothes and a thick, curly beard. He dressed simply, as a grave robber might.

Simone took the man's knife and held it in her open palm in front of him. "Where did you find this?"

"It was given to me," the man grunted. "Please, call for help."

April threw him a firm look. "Tell us who you are and we will."

"Please," he begged, coughing blood. "Call an ambulance. Please, miss. I need one."

Simone saw a darkness pooling around the man's wound. "He's bleeding a lot," she said to April.

"Tell us who you are," April said again. "Then we'll help you. Not before then."

"Help me and I will tell you everything!"

The man grunted once more, his eyes slamming shut and his body stiffening as a jolt of agony ripped through him.

"April…" Simone turned to her. "He's hurt pretty bad."

April did not remove her eyes from the man, almost daring him to give in. "Then he better tell us who he is and why he's here." She leaned closer. "I don't appreciate being shot at."

"Oh God, please-"

The injured man buckled, his torso lurching forward as another cry of anguish filled the chamber. He held his hands against his stomach, sweat pouring from his forehead.

"Come on, April," Simone said. "He can barely speak."

"Let him try one more time."

"April-"

"Stop!" April's head turned sharply to Simone, her icy blue eyes wide with hot anger. "If he's hurt that badly, he'll tell us what we want to know." She turned her burning glare back to the man. "Who are you, and why are you here? Speak."

The veins in the man's neck bulged, his jaw clenched tightly. Labored breaths came in sharp rasps. The blood around his stomach continued to spill, not only from the exit wound but also from the back. The crimson-black liquid pooled beneath the man, spreading across the floor.

Simone pulled her boot away before the man's blood reached it.

"I'm calling an ambulance," she said and turned for the stairs.

April stopped her with a hand on her shoulder. "No."

The two women locked eyes.

"He's going to die if we don't do something," Simone pleaded.

April did not react to her words.

"I'm making the call," Simone said. "Don't stop me."

Simone turned for the door but felt April's grip firm around her upper arm.

"What the hell's going on?" Lincoln said as he approached the standoff, returning from above soaking wet from the continued rain.

Simone shrugged free and went through the door and up the stairs.

Topside, she stood in the rain and made the emergency call on her phone. She wasn't sure how much information to give, so she told the operator that cries of pain were coming out of the ground near the Saint James Church. Only after she said the words did she realize how unholy and demonic it sounded.

But that wasn't too far removed from how she felt.

Lincoln and April emerged from below just as the call ended.

The trio hurried through the steady rain, back toward their apartment.

As April passed by, Simone noticed she carried the man's ornate knife.

"What did you do?" Simone asked.

April shoved the knife in her belt. "Forget it."

Simone caught up to April. "Tell me what you did."

"Nothing," April said in tones of admission. "I left him there like you wanted. He didn't say shit."

To Simone, the words rang with honesty. She trusted April about as much as she could under the circumstances.

Exactly how much she should trust her, however, was a thought that kept returning to Simone as they walked through the downpour.

* * *

"There was a second person," Lincoln said as he kicked off his boots inside the apartment.

April crossed to the kitchen area and wrung her sopping wet hair out in the sink. "Did you see them?"

He shook his head. "It was too dark. All I got was a silhouette. Male, thirties or forties, tall, curly hair and a beard. That's all I'm sure of."

Once her hair was dry enough, April crossed to the living area and threw the knife down on the table at the center of the room.

"We found a wooden crate," Simone said to her. "It was empty by the time we found it. Could that have been inside?"

April shook her head with confidence. "It's just a knife."

"Then why did you take it?"

April turned a firm look to Simone. "Because it's the only goddamn clue we have after three months of gathering intel. While you were vacationing in the mountains, some of us were trying to find a lead big enough to follow, and that lead walked out of the ossuary with a bigger advantage than we have. I wasn't leaving without something."

"That doesn't mean you had to torture the guy," Simone said to April's face, not backing down from the confrontation.

Lincoln stepped between them, arms spread to keep them apart. "Ladies, take a breather, all right? We're on the same damn side."

"Are we?" Simone asked. "You spend a quarter of a year gathering intel but can't even drop me a hint as to what I'm getting myself into before flying off to who knows where to do who knows what. If you want me on your side, you guys have to start telling me what the hell is going on. I'm not some benchwarmer you call in when you feel like it. If you want me to be a part of the team, then *let me be a part of the team*. Fill me in on what I'm here for and what we're doing."

It all came flooding out of Simone, the frustration and disappointment of her assignment, her role in all of it. The distrust being allowed to build through secrecy and militaristic protocol. She let herself have a moment to properly compose her next thought.

She took a calming breath. "I'm not here to torture information out of people, or pick up a gun and start shooting. I'm okay with going home right now if that's why you called for me. Just be honest and say so."

An instant of silence fell between the trio. At the end of it, April stormed away and shut herself in one of the bedrooms.

Simone let her arms fall in disappointment.

"That's not why you're here," Lincoln said as he approached her. "This expedition is a multi-step process, and we didn't want to pull you away from what you were doing until it mattered enough to do that. It was *my* decision, Simone. That's why I went to find you by myself. Clark has been eager to have you back ever since you left the base in California, but I did my best to convince him to give you some time to yourself. It wasn't easy, but I did it anyway because I trusted that was what you wanted. If that was wrong, then-"

"You weren't wrong," she said. "I'm sorry. But this ends now, the secrets. You tell me what we're doing here, what we're after, and where we're going next, or I will board the next plane out of here, and I am not joking."

"I understand," Lincoln said.

Simone stepped toward the bedroom she was assigned, but stopped halfway and turned back to Lincoln. "And don't make my decisions for me again. Let me make up my own mind."

"I apologize for that."

"Apology accepted." She started for the bedroom again, yet stopped short once more. "And Lincoln…"

He turned back toward her.

"Thank you for giving me time to myself," she said.

She left him with a little smile of recognition before entering her bedroom and closing the door behind her.

Simone changed into dry clothes, something comfortable enough for sleep should she find any that evening. Shorts and a tank top. She let her hair down and collapsed on the bed, as wide awake as ever.

The combination of her natural insomnia and the nightmarish visions of the terrors she'd experienced in Mexico was a wicked mistress. Sleep or not, neither outcome was desirable.

The only thing that seemed to help was the influence of alcohol or painkillers. Sometimes, it took both.

She'd taken several airplane bottles of liquor from the flight over. That night, she chose vodka. Straight. It burned going down the first few sips, but after she had a good buzz going, it was hardly a bad experience at all.

Relaxed on the bed, Simone stared up at the ceiling, wishing there was a way to sleep without closing her eyes. She knew that if it wasn't Heather or the man she'd shot greeting her in the darkness of slumber, it would be the man down in the ossuary who'd been impaled on an old bone fragment. She hoped the ambulance arrived in time.

Hours passed, and her bottle of vodka was long dry. She thought about cracking another open, but didn't want to run through the stash too quickly. There was no telling how long she'd be stuck on this expedition to find the Fallen Star - if it even existed.

Finally, she got up from bed and left the room for the kitchen with a few pills in her hand. She hadn't counted.

At the sink, Simone threw the painkillers in her mouth and ran her lips under the faucet, not stopping until she swallowed them all.

She shut the water off, wiping her mouth and turning to find Lincoln standing next to her.

"Sneak up on me, why don't you," she said as her heart rate quickened and then fell back down to normal.

"I figured you'd be awake." His eyes fell to the hand which had previously held Simone's painkillers. "Sleeping pills?"

Simone looked away with guilt and shrugged. "They help me sleep sometimes." She chose not to correct him on what type of pills she had taken.

Lincoln took a glass from the cabinet and filled it with water from the faucet. "Want to sit with me?"

"Sure," Simone said. She followed him to the living area. He took the couch, she took the love seat.

Lincoln sipped his water. "For my own personal assurance, you are good, right?"

Simone's eyes narrowed at the suspicious inquiry. "What do you mean?"

"I mean - and don't take this personally - I mean you only take sleeping pills to sleep, right?"

Simone leaned back. "That's kind of a personal question."

Lincoln drank again, then set his glass on the table between them. "All I'm saying is that this line of work can change people. I've seen it before. Some of the stuff we come across … there's no easy way to process that. We've had people who weren't fit for it, and they often chose the self-medicating route."

"Do you think I'm fit for it?" Simone asked - a question she would have kept to herself had she been more clear-headed and well-rested.

"I don't know. Are you?"

She wanted to say yes, but she didn't want to lie. "I'm here, aren't I?"

"You are."

"Then I'm good."

Lincoln finished his water and set the empty glass down. "I don't know where the next leg of the journey takes us, but if you want to talk about anything…"

"I'm fine," Simone said.

Lincoln shrugged. "You said you want to be included. I'm including you. It's not an easy job, what we do. None of us can do it on our own. The hunt itself, or the … you know … other part."

Simone knew he meant the moral quandaries of taking human life and the intense mental stress of nearly having her own life taken from her, but he seemed just as afraid to say so as she was.

Everyone dealt with it in their own way. It seemed to manifest in April as violent determination. Simone's own method was, indeed, self-medication. She wasn't sure which was more unhealthy.

"Thanks," was all she said, knowing he meant well. "I should try to get some sleep."

"Me, too."

They each stood, exchanged an awkward grin in the dark, and retreated to their beds.

Simone lay awake yet again, studying the pattern of paint on the ceiling as the painkillers began to take effect.

8.

Skarstind Mountain, Norway

On the fourth day of his climb, Solomon began entertaining thoughts of abandoning his ascent, packing up, and heading back down the mountain.

He hadn't realized just how difficult a task it was to climb the Skarstind Mountains. He wasn't a great climber, but he was resilient, and he expected the same from Simone. He didn't know a great deal about her physical training other than she had been a very decorated athlete in track and field competitions before entering the world of treasure hunting and exploration.

She was well-conditioned for a harsh and demanding task. Solomon considered that an advantage. He didn't have the same regimen, the history of always being active. He'd spent a lot of time in intelligence gathering operations with SWANN under Heather Severn before branching out into field work. That was only two years back. His body wasn't accustomed to climbing snowy mountains and trekking through the wilderness.

But the one advantage Solomon had over Simone was the element of surprise.

With help from Lilly, he could find out whatever he needed to know about Simone. He was a few steps behind, but not for long. Each new piece of data he gathered led him closer to Simone. Once he knew what she knew, there was no way to stop him from setting up his sniper rifle from two hundred yards away and picking her off before she had a chance to hear the shot.

The thought gave Solomon the strength he needed to push forward one more day, to follow the tracks in the path to whatever Simone had been looking for.

Later that afternoon, he found it.

A peaceful little log cabin with a smoking chimney, nestled in the midst of snow-capped evergreens. It looked like something from a storybook.

Solomon approached the front door and gave a knock.

The door swung open after a minute and there stood an elderly man whose smile of expectation faded almost instantaneously as his eyes met with Solomon's.

"Can I help you?" the old man asked.

Solomon shook the snow from his rented parka. "May I come inside, please? It's awfully cold out here."

"Of course, of course." The old man stepped aside for Solomon to enter.

"Thank you."

The warmth from the wood stove had Solomon sweating. He began to remove his outdoor gear.

"What brings you this far out?" the old man asked.

"It is pretty far out," Solomon said, putting his hat, gloves, and scarf aside. "Do you get many visitors up here?"

"No, not many. Let me take your coat."

Solomon handed him the parka. "Anyone stop by recently?"

The old man turned for the coat rack but stopped suddenly upon hearing the question. He held the parka in his hands, feeling the texture, studying the pattern as if had had seen it recently.

He hung the coat up and turned to Solomon. "May I ask who you are, young man?"

Only after the words had been spoken did he see the gun in Solomon's hand.

"No, you may not," Solomon said, gun held on the old man. "I'm the one who will be asking the questions. All you have to do is answer."

The old man swallowed but held his ground. He straightened himself, keeping his eyes locked on his adversary. "Are you going to shoot me?"

"You're not too good at this, I see." Solomon stepped between the door and the old man to cut off the nearest exit. With the gun, he motioned for an old rocking chair. "Have a seat."

The old man obeyed, sitting down with his head held high.

Solomon sat on the table at the center of the room, gun held on the old man the entire time. "You had a visitor recently. A woman. Late twenties, tall, athletic, long dark hair. Answers to the name Simone Winifred Cassidy."

The color drained from the old man's face, but he said nothing. He didn't have to. Solomon knew he was right.

"She went out of her way to pay you a visit, is that right?"

The old man's chest rose and fell with a deep, slow, steady breath. He remained silent.

"Is it?" Solomon said in a demanding tone.

"She's not here, if that's what you're getting at," the old man said.

"I know she's not here. It's just you and me. Nobody else for miles and miles around." Solomon leaned a bit closer. "Why was she here, old timer?"

"You're going to shoot me whether I tell you or not. If that's the case, just go ahead and do it. I don't have much time left, anyhow."

"That's not true," Solomon said. "You have plenty of time to tell me what I'd like to know."

"And what would you like to know?"

"Tell me why you received a surprise visit from Simone Winifred Cassidy."

"And what are you going to do with that information?" the old man asked. "She came for my root vegetable stew recipe, and I told her I'm taking it to the grave with me. And that goes for you, too, young man."

A grin spread across Solomon's face. "Well, then I'm afraid I'll have to be on my way."

He stood, tucking the gun in the back of his waistband.

"It's a real shame I came all this way for nothing."

He turned toward the coat rack, then stopped. Turning back, he said. "Oh, wait. There is one other thing…"

The old man watched as Solomon sat again on the table. His eyes widened with a terror he was trying his best to suppress. He swallowed hard, his hands gripping the arms of the chair. But the gun remained out of Solomon's hands.

"I didn't come here to hurt you," Solomon said. "I came here to warn you."

"Warn me?" the old man said in confusion.

Solomon nodded. "That's right. I wanted to warn you that Simone Winifred Cassidy may not be the person she's claiming to be."

The old man's eyes narrowed. "What do you mean? What are you getting at?"

"You know who she's working for, right? A man named Clark Bannicheck."

"Yes, I know." The old man's voice took on a distressed quality, as if giving the answer with great reluctance.

"What do you know about him?"

"I know enough," and the old man left it at that.

"It sounds to me like you don't approve of the arrangement," Solomon said, trying to play on the old man's emotions to get him to spill something, some key bit of information that Solomon could run with.

"I … I don't … Who are you?" the old man stammered.

"Clark is a smart man. He wouldn't think twice about sending her up here unless it was worth the time and effort. You think I came here to grill you for information? No, that's why *she* came here."

The old man huffed. "She didn't come brandishing a gun."

"No," Solomon said. "She came as a friend. Isn't that right? And I bet you played right into it, maybe even feeding her some of your famous root vegetable stew."

The old man's eyes darted back and forth. A conflict was brewing in his head, Solomon could sense it. He only knew the name Clark Bannicheck from the last mission in Mexico, but he hung it out on a line and the old man ate it up like bait.

"You probably warned her about him, didn't you?" Solomon continued. "Warned her that working together could be dangerous. Because you know him. And what was the pretense that brought her here in the first place? I'm guessing it had something to do with her parents. What were their names?" He thought back to the names he'd read while skimming through their journal. "Dominic and Citra?"

"Enough!" The old man pushed himself to his feet, his eyes burning hotter than the coals in the fireplace. "I don't know who you are or what your agenda is, but you can see yourself out."

Solomon rose to his feet, eye to eye with the old man. "Sit back down. I'm not ready to leave."

"I don't care what you're ready for," the old man said. "Take your things and get out!" He flung out his arm toward the door.

He then looked down at the gun barrel pressed against his stomach.

"Sit. Down."

Solomon didn't repeat himself again. The old man slowly returned himself to the rocking chair.

Solomon sank back down to his seat on the table, gun held forward once more to prevent any more outbursts.

"Very good," Solomon said. "Now, where were we?"

The old man clenched his jaw, electing not to answer.

"You're a friend of theirs, is that right?" Solomon asked. "Simone's parents. How did you know them?"

The old man sat still and silent, as stubborn as a mule.

Solomon sighed. "I said I didn't come here to hurt you." He turned the gun over in his hands, eyes cast down to study the deadly weapon. He then raised his glare up to the old man. "But I didn't say I wouldn't."

The old man steeled himself, readying both physically and mentally for whatever punishment Solomon was about to inflict.

Clearing his throat, the old man said, "Well then, what are you waiting for?"

9.

Brno, Czech Republic

Simone was sitting cross-legged on the couch, eating a bowl of cereal when April strolled sleepily out from her bedroom.

"Morning," Simone said between spoonfuls.

Rubbing sleep from her squinting eyes, April blinked rapidly and searched for a clock. "What time is it?"

"Almost five," Simone said.

"Jesus. You really don't sleep."

Simone shook her head. "I got enough. What are you doing up so early?"

April raised her hand to reveal the dagger taken from the injured man in the ossuary. "Clark should be getting back to me about this." She sat on a chair near the couch. "I sent over some photos last night. He said he'd run it through the database and see what came back. It usually takes a while."

Simone finished her breakfast and set the bowl aside. "Look, I wanted to apologize for last night."

"Don't," April said. Simone expected more, but that's all she had to say.

An awkward silence fell between them, punctuated by the stillness of the early morning's lack of activity surrounding their little apartment building. The city still slept.

"So," Simone said to further the conversation. "What do you do when you're not doing ... this?"

April raised her sleepy, squinting eyes to Simone. "What are we, friends now?"

She stood and padded into the bathroom. Seconds later, Simone heard the shower running.

I guess not, Simone thought.

Getting information out of April was like pulling a jaguar's teeth without pliers or a sedative. It could probably be done, but was it worth the effort?

They weren't friends. They were just co-workers. That was all. Once the job was done, they wouldn't hang out, go for brunch, call each other on the phone. Simone always enjoyed getting to know the people she worked with, and the urge to do that had been nagging at her ever since Harald issued the warning about Clark.

Simone felt like throwing the empty cereal bowl at the bathroom door, but elected not to. It was frustrating to work with people like April, who had the job set in their mind, that it had to be done their way, and discussion on the matter only resulted in a conflict that could be avoided by simply going along with them.

But that wasn't Simone's style.

She didn't follow blindly. She liked to ask questions, to see if there was a better way, a safer way, a more expedient way. More and more, April was reminding Simone of the Frenchman she'd worked with in Cambodia, whose headstrong ways ultimately led to his demise.

She hoped April's hot-headedness didn't come back to haunt her.

As Simone sat on the couch, thoughts of her parents circled around in her head. She had so much more to learn, and sitting here in the Czech Republic felt as if she was wasting time. April was showering while waiting for contact from Clark so they could find out the origin of the knife taken from the injured man, but there was another way.

Simone didn't want to entertain the idea that the man's life had been spared simply because she was there. Had it been April by herself, would she have tortured him to death just for information?

Simone shook her head and rubbed her face, thinking about who she was working for and how she ever allowed herself to get caught up with people like April Farren.

When she was finished with her early breakfast, Simone got dressed, laced up her boots, tied her hair back, and exited the apartment before April's shower was done.

Hunching her shoulders, Simone strolled through the dim and grey morning. The sun was still on the rise, and a chill clung to the air, but she was happy to be out of the apartment. The tiny bedroom had her running in circles, and being unable to sleep only exacerbated the feeling that she had to get out and do something.

The quicker they found the Fallen Star, the quicker she could get back to Norway, pack up whatever she was willing to take with her, and follow her parents' writing to the next leg of the journey, wherever that might be.

The man they'd found injured in the ossuary would have survived. She'd made the call quickly enough and they had heard the ambulance siren as they'd walked away through the rain. The injury didn't appear fatal, but looked serious enough. That meant he would have been taken to a hospital nearby where he would no doubt have stayed the night.

Simone consulted her phone for area hospitals. If she could find the man and convince him to give her some information, they wouldn't have to wait for Clark to call back.

Strolling down the cobbled streets, Simone felt more like a secret agent than a treasure hunter, off on a covert mission to extract intel from a target.

She almost laughed at the absurdity. *A secret agent. No chance in hell.*

* * *

Simone checked three hospitals before deciding to give up. Lincoln had already texted her, asking where she went off to. He said nothing of Clark giving new intel, or that she had to come back right away to catch a flight to who knows where.

The city was awakening now, and how quickly the world became alive around her reminded Simone that Brno was the second largest city in the Czech Republic. It was starting to feel that way.

Morning was still young. She had rented a bicycle for journeying through the city and wasn't ready to take it back just yet. With no pressing news from the apartment, Simone changed her mind about giving up and started off toward the next hospital on her list.

It didn't take long to get there - or at least it didn't feel like it did. But when Simone checked the time, she saw that she'd been cycling for nearly half an hour.

Still no word from Lincoln, April, or Clark. She replied that she went out for fresh air, then locked up the bike and went inside the Czech Medical Center.

"Do you speak English?" Simone asked as she approached the front desk.

The young man behind the counter nodded. "Yes, I am fluent."

He wore thick glasses and a spotless white coat. To Simone's eyes, he looked more like a student than an employee. He must have been fresh out of university.

Simone leaned against the counter and mentally prepared her speech. She'd had three opportunities to work out the bugs in her attempt to extract intel, and she felt confident that she could appear more natural this time.

"I'm wondering if you could help me," she said. "I'm looking for a man who might have come in last night. He's roughly my age, my height. Has a beard. He was impaled by a bone fragment through the abdomen."

The young man typed something on his computer. "Who may I ask is inquiring?"

"I am a private investigator," Simone said.

The young man typed some more, clicked his mouse a few times. Simone leaned on the counter, trying to look nonchalant - how she pictured a real PI might stand.

"Uh, we do have an injury similar to the one you described," the young desk attendant said.

"Do you have a name?"

The young man hesitated. "Uh, I'm not sure if I could give you that information, miss…?"

Oh crap, he wants my *name.* "You can call me Miss Munroe," Simone said, picking the first name that she could think of. "Miss Rosa Munroe. Private investigator," she added for emphasis.

"Miss Munroe, I…" the young man said with an uncertain head shake.

Simone leaned in closer and lowered her voice to a conspiratorial whisper. "I hope you understand that this is a sensitive matter, and other people's lives are depending on this man. I'm going to need you to tell me his name and what room I can find him in."

She held her eyes on his, not blinking, not pulling away. The eye contact made the young man look away nervously. He looked to his computer screen, his hands, the floor, everywhere but Simone's unflinching stare.

"How about this," she said in compromise. "You can walk over to that water fountain…" She pointed. "And grab a quick drink. By the time you get back, I'll be gone. It'll be like I was never here, and you don't have to show me anything."

The young man looked up upon hearing the proposition. Slowly, he nodded. Without a word, he rose from his seat and shuffled toward the water fountain.

Simone gave a quick glance and saw that nobody was watching. She leaned around to glimpse the screen, searched as fast as she could for the box where the patient's name would be, found the room number, and stepped away from the counter as if nothing wrong had happened.

By the time the young desk attendant turned around, Simone was gone.

She rode the elevator to the third floor where the patient Ahmed Haddad was being kept. She made her way down the hallway to room 307. Before entering, Simone took a deep breath, then pushed the door open and stepped inside.

He was the only patient in the room. Even with the sheets pulled up to his shoulders, Simone could see the heavy wrapping of bandages around his stomach.

Simone eased herself into the chair next to his bedside. His eyes flickered open, taking a moment to adjust to the light in the room.

"Good morning," Simone said.

"Who … who are you?" Ahmed's voice was dry and cracked. He could barely get any words out.

Simone poured a glass of water and handed it to the man. Slowly, he raised an unsteady hand and took it. He brought it to his parched lips and sipped the smallest sip. Simone took the glass and set it aside.

"Do you remember me?" she asked.

Ahmed nodded a sluggish nod. "You are the one who called for help. You rescued me, and now you sit by my bed. I understand none of this."

"What's not to understand?"

"Unless you are here to kill me," he said. "Why else would you be here at your enemy's bedside?"

Simone squinted at him. "Enemy? Who says I'm your enemy?"

Ahmed chuckled. "Who do you think was shooting at your friend? The one with the fire in her hair and the ink on her arms."

Simone studied the man as recognition set in. "It was you that shot? It wasn't your partner who ran out and left you there?"

"He made it safely away. That is all that matters."

Simone's jaw hung open. "All that matters? You nearly died!"

"And I would die for the Prince a thousand times if I could," Ahmed said. "I was granted one life on this world, and you have left me alive to give it another day. For that, I thank you."

Not believing what she heard, Simone considered how many drugs the man must have been on.

"You, too, know what secrets were kept in the crypt." Ahmed coughed. "I expect you were there for the same reason. I do not know what else would drive you to such a place after dark."

Simone hesitated. "The Fallen Star?"

Ahmed scoffed. "One could wish the Fallen Star to be so easy to locate, but wishing does not make it true."

"What would make it true?" Simone asked. "Whatever was in the crate on the altar?"

For the first time, Ahmed smiled. "I can say no more to you. The fate of the Fallen Star is in greater hands now. There is nothing you can do."

Simone leaned back in her chair. The direct approach wouldn't work, she knew. She had to be more indirect. If this man was going to give out any more information, it wouldn't be voluntarily.

She thought back to April's method of torturing a dying man. Even that did not work. He would have accepted a painful, prolonged death rather than tell April what he found. His devotion was strong. Stronger than brute force. Stronger than the will to live.

Simone had no idea what to say, so she played the only card she had.

"We have your knife," she said.

Ahmed's eyes shifted to Simone. "The knife your friend stole from me?"

"She's not my friend," Simone said, recalling April's words. "I was forced to work with her," she continued. "To tell you the truth, I don't like it very much. I disagree with her methods. We don't get along too well. I probably won't be working with her after this job is done."

Ahmed turned a curious look to Simone. "Forced to work together?"

Simone exhaled a sigh. "They tricked me, she and the people she works for. They didn't tell me where we were going or what they wanted me to do." She leaned forward. "I'm an explorer, not a thief. I shouldn't be crawling through a burial chamber. There are places in the world nobody's been to yet, places that haven't been seen in hundreds - no, *thousands* of years. I should be out there. Instead, here I am."

Simone finished her rant with a long inhale and a deep exhale. There must have been some truth showing in her speech, some unexpected display of honesty, because Ahmed was sitting up, eyes fixed on Simone.

"In my country," Ahmed said, "women do not enjoy the rights you have. If you can leave, why don't you leave?"

"Leave here?" Simone asked.

Ahmed nodded. "Your friend seems like the dangerous type. Would she kill you if you tried to leave?"

"No, it's not like that," Simone said. "I mean, the company is well-funded and well-armed, and they might not particularly enjoy it if I just quit in the middle of an expedition, but I don't know if they'd kill me."

Ahmed raised his hand in the direction of the glass of water. Simone gave it to him once again. He sipped and handed it back.

"And she's not my friend," Simone added, setting the glass aside.

"If you say so," Ahmed said.

Simone relaxed in the chair. "Your knife is quite impressive. The detail is impeccable. I'll see what I can do to get it back to you."

"It was a gift from Prince Orimer Kamal himself," Ahmed said. "I would appreciate it greatly if you could see it returned to me."

"I have to wonder what you'd have to do for such a gift."

Simone had never heard the name Prince Orimer Kamal before in her life, but gave no indication to Ahmed, deciding it was better that not every detail of her knowledge be revealed right away.

"I'm not sure if you would find the story appealing," he said. "It is quite long and filled with many squeamish moments. But if the tale may result in the gift's return, then I suppose it must be told."

"I have time," Simone said as she threaded her fingers together in her lap.

10.

Dubai, United Arab Emirates

Prince Orimer Kamal nearly gagged as he watched the Rolls-Royce Phantom pull up to where he was standing outside the Dubai International Airport.

That bastard, Murad, he thought. *Always trying to prove something.*

The chauffeur got out and rounded the automobile to open the door for Prince Kamal to get inside.

Prince Kamal's two servants loaded the luggage and got in beside him. Before he knew it, they were on their way to meet with Murad Abdullah.

The thought twisted Prince Kamal's stomach. He wanted to tell the driver to pull over so he could retch on their sidewalk. Better yet, he could spew his vomit all over the luxurious interior of the Rolls-Royce.

Murad Abdullah, never wasting an opportunity to shove in the Saudi Prince's face how superior he felt his country to be. Why else would he insist on meeting at the Burj Al Arab? The man owned enough property of his own to house a small army if need be.

No, this meeting was less about discussing the whereabouts of the Fallen Star and more of a display of Dubai's unsurpassed magnificence.

The Rolls-Royce turned down a narrow road that led out to where the world's only seven-star hotel sat on the waters of the Persian Gulf.

The chauffeur brought the car to a stop and got out to open the door for Prince Kamal. The two servants took care of the luggage. Prince Kamal did not even lift a finger.

Stepping out of the vehicle, the Prince gazed upon one of the most iconic structures of the Middle East, and perhaps even the world.

"You will find Mr. Abdullah at the Al Muntaha. Twenty-seventh floor," said the chauffeur with a bow.

Prince Kamal barely grunted in reply. The servants brought the luggage inside as the Prince stood before the building - an admittedly stunning feat of engineering - as he felt a sour taste rise up in the back of his throat.

Of all the weapons dealers…

Prince Kamal didn't know why he was stuck doing business with the likes of Murad Abdullah, but there was no other man on the planet who not only wanted what he had, and not only had the wealth and resources the Prince wanted, but was also willing to pay.

Prince Kamal spat on the ground, straightened the sleeves of his spotless white robe, and strode inside.

* * *

"I trust that you have what we discussed," Murad Abdullah said in greeting Prince Kamal.

It wasn't much of a greeting, seeing that Murad failed to rise from his seat or even stop chewing his mouthful of food.

Prince Kamal knew the insult was intended. A friend would have waited for all parties to arrive before ordering. A true friend would have ordered for him.

Murad had food only for himself. He did not offer the Prince a menu.

"I do," Prince Kamal said as a servant pulled out a chair for him to sit. To the servant, he said, "The scroll."

The servant handed Prince Kamal a metal tube.

Murad stopped chewing. "The Star is in there? I expected it to be bigger."

"Not the Star," the Prince said.

He twisted off the end of the tube and gave it a shake. A rolled-up piece of parchment fell onto the table before him.

Murad leaned in to study the mysterious scroll. His eyes lifted to Prince Kamal. "This is not the Fallen Star."

"It is, in fact, not the Fallen Star," Prince Kamal said "But it will get you there."

Murad snapped back in his seat and drank from his wine goblet. Wiping his mouth, he said, "Prince Kamal, are you going back on the deal we agreed upon-"

"The deal was that I help you locate the Fallen Star. I have fulfilled my end of the bargain." He held a hand out over the scroll to indicate the evidence.

Murad ate the last scraps of food. "Do you know what I have before me?" he asked.

"You have everything you need to find the Fallen Star."

Murad lifted his empty plate and let it drop to the table in a metallic cacophony. "I have nothing! Do you see the Fallen Star before me, Prince? Because I do not."

"The deal was that I-"

"The deal was an exchange. You hand me the Fallen Star, then I ship you a crate of missiles. I don't care what you do with them any more than I care about where the Fallen Star exists today, at this very moment. What I care about is having it in my possession. Which part of the deal is confusing to you?"

Prince Kamal leveled at Murad a glare of brimstone. He wished he could reach across the table and strangle the man with his bare hands. Having his servants do it wouldn't bring the same level of satisfaction as feeling the breath building up in the man's throat, unable to escape.

But he knew that he would be the very next person on the planet to die should he risk an attempt on Murad's life. He doubted he could choke the man to death in the time it would take any of the half dozen armed guards in the room to shoot him with a marksman's precision. He would die first, and Murad would walk out of the Al Muntaha with the scroll detailing the whereabouts of the Fallen Star without having to give up any weapons for it.

Prince Kamal knew he had to control his anger. He thought about what he had and what Murad wanted. He had an ancient scroll that could take Murad straight to the Fallen Star, but that was not what Murad wanted. He wanted the object for himself. He didn't want to work for it, he wanted to barter for it.

And that was where Prince Kamal had an advantage.

"Fine," he said. "I will bring you the Fallen Star and hand it to you myself."

Murad smiled a wide smile. "Very good."

"As long as the conditions of our deal are fulfilled."

Murad lurched forward, arms spread. "Do you take me for a man who goes back on a business deal? Prince, you do not even know me. I resent the accusation."

Prince Kamal held out his palms, urging peace. "There is no accusation to resent, old friend. Our deal did not stipulate that I hand the object to you, only that I help you find it." He tapped on the scroll. "I have helped you find it. If you would like to renegotiate the contract, I would be happy to oblige."

Murad slammed back another swig of wine. "Renegotiate," he said, the word sounding like venom on his tongue. "Fine. You bring me the Fallen Star, place it in my hand. I will increase your order by ten percent."

"Twenty."

"Fifteen."

"Twenty," Prince Kamal said with a new-found confidence. He knew he held the bargaining power. He knew Murad would bend. He didn't do it easily, but he would not pass up the opportunity to possess one of the most sought-after relics in the archaeological community.

Murad huffed in displeasure. "Fine, twenty percent. But no more."

Prince Kamal stood, drawing his robe tighter across his stomach. "Murad, we have a deal." He held out a hand for Murad to shake.

After a moment of contemplation, Murad rose and shook the Prince's hand. Prince Kamal turned to leave, but found his hand still held firm in Murad's grip.

"In one week, the bonus drops to fifteen. Two weeks, ten. Three weeks, you find yourself another buyer."

Prince Kamal's red-hot stare burned into Murad. He wrenched his hand free. "I will return within one week."

"Good," said Murad. "However, I will hold off on informing my buyers until you deliver the artifact. It's not that I don't trust you, of course."

Prince Kamal gave a short laugh. "Your little auction will not be delayed, I assure you."

"Auction?" Murad said with an ever-widening smile. "See, Prince, that is where you and I are fundamentally different. Until you start to see the bigger picture, you will always be the one stuck running around to dig up old gemstones instead of the one making a fortune from someone else's effort. You should ask yourself why I would wish to sell the Fallen Star to one buyer when I can smash it into little pieces and sell each fragment for the price of the whole thing."

Prince Kamal narrowed his eyes at Murad. "You would destroy it?"

Murad shrugged. "It's an old rock. It means nothing to me. But I hope it means enough for you to deliver it in one piece. Otherwise, you would find yourself on the wrong end of my arsenal. Are we at an understanding?"

Prince Kamal gave a slow nod. "I will see it delivered to you, personally."

The Prince strode toward the exit with his two servants, choosing not to voice his plans aloud.

Before placing the Fallen Star into Murad's hand, he would have some additional demands that needed to be met. Otherwise, no deal.

He was a Saudi Prince. Murad's goons couldn't touch him any more than he could touch Murad. They had to barter like businessmen, and Murad wanted the Fallen Star more than the Prince wanted weapons. He could get weapons elsewhere. Using the Fallen Star was simply an easier and cheaper method.

Consulting the old scroll on his ride down the elevator, Prince Orimer Kamal considered how simple it was, playing Murad the way he did. He figured he could get the bonus up to fifty percent before all was said and done.

It was shaping up to be the simplest weapons deal he had ever secured.

11.

Brno, Czech Republic

"Where the hell have you been?"

April jumped to her feet and marched toward the door as Simone entered. By the tone of her voice, Simone figured that Clark had got in touch at some point while she was gone.

"Sorry, I needed some fresh air," Simone said.

"Yeah?" April asked with sarcasm lacing the word. "Well, you'll get plenty. Pack your stuff and get ready to leave. Plane will be here any minute."

Simone stepped around April, who refused to move from where she stood blocking the path to the kitchen area. "My things are packed."

She filled a glass of water and slowly drank the entire thing.

Lincoln entered the room, toting his luggage. He set it down near the door. "We've got a lead on the knife you found in the ossuary."

"Let me guess," Simone said as she washed the empty glass. "We're off to Dubai."

"Guess again," said April.

"Saudi Arabia," Lincoln said, his tone seeking to douse the fires of conflict between the two women.

Simone shut off the flow of water at the sink. "Says who?"

"Says Clark," April said. "His call came in while you were out getting your morning coffee or whatever. The inscription and designs on the hilt are the symbol of the royal Kamal family. Of Saudi Arabia, not Dubai."

"It's like a trademark," Lincoln added. "Used most notably by Prince Orimer Kamal."

Simone dried the newly clean glass and put it back in the cabinet. She closed the door and turned around, leaning against the sink on both palms.

"Let me guess ... Prince Orimer Kamal offered the knife we have in our possession to a man named Ahmed Haddad for helping secure a defense contract with a weapons dealer named Murad Abdullah. It was primarily for communications and cyber-security technology to sell to the Pentagon. Because of his work in closing that deal, Ahmed was given the task of recovering the Fallen Star to bring to Prince Kamal so he could sell it to Murad Abdullah for an even larger cache of arms - also for sale to the Pentagon."

April and Lincoln exchanged a look of amazement.

Simone continued, "So, why would we go to Saudi Arabia if Prince Kamal is currently in Dubai meeting with Murad Abdullah?"

April stepped forward, her face twisted into something between astonishment and displeasure. "How the hell do you know this?"

Simone fixed her glare directly into April's blazing blue eyes. "It's amazing what you can accomplish by helping people instead of hurting them."

"Okay," Lincoln said, sensing the rage boiling over inside April. He put a hand around her tattooed arm and tugged her away. "Let's get this gear ready for departure."

Simone kept her composure as April turned away with a huff of resentment. She knew she was right. She hadn't detected a hint of dishonesty from Ahmed. In fact, he seemed to share the same feelings toward April - that she was a loose cannon, someone who shouldn't be trusted. There was no telling exactly to what lengths she would go to finish a job.

Simone was scared to consider it. Always the first in the field, April often acted alone. With no one to reel her back in, what had she done, in the Czech Republic, Mexico, or anywhere, that had allowed their party to do what they did? How many people were hurt?

How many had to die?

First Harald's warning, then Ahmed's question. Why didn't Simone just split? She had her parents' travel journal. She had Harald. What else could Clark offer her that she couldn't find on her own?

"So," she said to Lincoln. "Where are we flying to?"

April carried her bags out of the room, leaving Lincoln and Simone alone.

Lincoln paused to think about his answer. "We have orders to go to Saudi Arabia."

"Then you can take off without me," Simone said.

The air left Lincoln's lungs in exasperation. He set his bags down. "Simone-"

"Don't do that," she said. "Don't try to convince me. I know I'm right, and I know that *you* know I'm right. I'm not going with you, Lincoln. It's a waste of time."

Lincoln brought a hand up and rubbed his face. His expression was close to one of physical pain. The look told Simone that he didn't think it should be so hard to work things out between them, and she agreed.

"Simone, what I was going to say is that we don't always have to follow orders."

Simone stepped away from the counter with an eagerness in her heart. "Well, then let's go to Dubai."

"The trouble," he said, "is that we have to convince April."

Simone held up her hands. "That's all on you. I'm sorry, but we're not exactly getting along very well right now. I don't know if you've noticed."

"That's why you have to do it," Lincoln said.

Simone blinked. "What?"

He leaned toward her, his eyes hard and cold. "Get along."

With that, he took his bags and left Simone standing in the apartment alone.

* * *

Simone was the last one to get to the plane. April was already on board. Once her things were loaded up, Simone climbed the steps into the plane and found April sitting there.

"April," Simone said. "Listen…"

"Save it." April didn't bother to look up. She kept her face down toward her phone.

Simone stood in the same spot, wondering what to do next. Was she convinced or not?

Lincoln boarded the plane. Simone stepped aside and took a seat so that Lincoln could do the same.

As the three of them sat, nobody exchanged a word. The pilot spoke over the intercom, announcing their change in destination.

They were going to Dubai.

Simone reclined her seat, hoping she was indeed right. She felt right, but if her instincts were wrong, the Fallen Star would be out of their hands, and likely for good.

She shut her eyes, contemplating what she considered to be her last journey for Clark Bannicheck. Once the Fallen Star was found and brought back to the States, that was it. She was done.

As the plane took off, Simone wondered why she hadn't walked away already, as the man in the hospital had suggested.

She didn't have an answer. Part of her wanted to split, but another part could never abandon a relic of that kind of significance, no matter what the working conditions were like.

As much as she wanted to believe she could tell Clark that she wouldn't be working for him again, Simone knew that saying something and actually doing it were two very different things.

* * *

Midway through the flight, Simone's phone rang.

Her eyes fluttered open. She hadn't been sleeping, although not for the lack of trying. Just resting her eyes.

She'd already finished two little bottles of gin and was working on a third, hoping it would be enough to put her to sleep for a few hours. It sounded good in theory, but failed to work in practice.

Simone retrieved the phone from her pocket and answered in a hushed voice, as she saw that April and Lincoln were both fast asleep. Often on these kinds of expeditions, travel was the only occasion that offered any sort of substantial rest.

"Hello?" Simone said. In her haste to answer and silence the ringtone, she didn't have a chance to look at the caller ID.

"Simone, it's me," said the voice of Georgia Gates.

Simone rubbed her eyes and spoke at a low volume. "What's up? What time is it?" she asked, not at once realizing they were several times zones apart. The booze had her mind operating slower than usual.

"Simone, can you talk? I don't have much time."

Georgia's voice was also low, and Simone didn't understand why.

"Sure, give me a second."

Simone got up from her seat and went to the plane's tiny restroom. Once the door was locked behind her, she sat down and cupped the phone as she held it close to her ear. "What is it?"

"Simone, I did some digging. The Serpent's Fang?"

Simone's heart rate quickened. "What about it? What did you find? Did you find it?"

"No, I didn't find squat," Georgia said. "I looked everywhere, in every archive, old and new just for the hell of it. There's no record anywhere. As far as I can tell, it's never been inventoried. Not here, not anywhere."

"You know what's in other museums?"

"Everything's accounted for, Simone. *Everything*. Except this Serpent's Fang you told me about. Are you sure that's what you found?"

"Ten-thousand percent positive," Simone said. "What about Clark Bannicheck? Did you come across that name?"

"Not at all," Georgia said. "This all sounds really strange, Simone. What is it that you're getting yourself into?"

"If I could tell you, I would. But I don't even know. If you can find anything else, let me know, but don't..."

"Don't what? Simone?" Georgia sounded overly concerned - not only for her well-being, but for the well-being of her closest friend.

"Don't get caught," Simone said.

Simone lowered the phone at the sound of a noise outside the door. She sat still, hand over her phone, listening...

After she was convinced nobody was out there, that neither April nor Lincoln had awakened, she brought the phone back to her ear. "Georgia, you still there?"

"I'm here, girl."

"Listen, thanks for looking into this for me. I owe you."

"You don't owe me a damn thing," Georgia said. "Because I didn't find a damn thing."

"You helped more than you realize," Simone said. "I gotta go. I'll be in touch."

Simone ended the call and exited the restroom.

In the aisle, she found Lincoln standing before her. Awake.

"All yours," Simone said, playing it off.

"Thanks," Lincoln said with sleep in his voice.

They awkwardly stepped around one another in the narrow space and Simone went back to her seat, wondering if Lincoln had heard her talking on the phone just then.

Simone drank more of the third gin bottle. The alcohol was doing nothing but getting her drunk. It didn't help put her to sleep. It had helped in the past, but she was building up a tolerance. It was taking more and more each time.

That's why she had begun mixing booze with painkillers. Neither one worked on its own unless she slammed so many that she woke up in a puddle of her own puke.

That couldn't happen, she knew. She had to be awake and ready for whatever they had to do in Dubai.

Everyone knew she had insomnia, but nobody knew what she did in her efforts to find that elusive sleep. Not even Georgia. Simone wondered if Lincoln had smelled the gin on her breath as they passed each other in the aisle.

Simone rested her eyes again, hoping and praying that she wasn't greeted by Heather's dying face for the hundredth time, that she didn't hear the shot she'd fired that took a man's life.

All she wanted to do was sleep.

12.

Dubai, United Arab Emirates

"Simone, time to wake up."

Simone startled awake at the sound of Lincoln's voice. Blinking her eyes open, she found herself staring up at his face as he stared down at her.

She wiped drool from the corner of her mouth and repositioned herself in the seat as a dull throb found its way to the back of her head. The light from the open door felt brighter than the sun.

"What happened?" Simone asked as she found herself wondering when she passed out and for how long.

"We landed," Lincoln said. "Let's go."

He turned away, his gaze lingering briefly on the five empty gin bottles on the seat next to Simone.

She didn't recall drinking the other two.

Simone rubbed her face and pushed herself to her feet. Her body ached, as if she hadn't slept at all. It felt as though she would have been better off staying awake the entire flight.

Stepping off the plane, she shielded her eyes from the relentlessly bright morning, thinking about where she packed her hat and if it was easy enough to get to quickly.

April approached where Simone stood with Lincoln. "Prince Kamal?" she asked.

"That's him," Simone said. Her mouth felt drier then the sand that surrounded the city.

"He's staying at Atlantis The Palm, and I don't expect for long," April said.

Simone pulled her hat from her luggage and put it on, not asking how April knew what she knew. She was good at finding people, and was no doubt aided by Clark's exceptional pool of resources. Simone wondered if someone had to be bribed for the information on Prince Kamal, who didn't sound like an easy man to target.

"What are you thinking?" Lincoln asked April.

"I'm thinking we better stop wasting time talking about it and start moving." April started walking away. "I'll get us a rental."

Rental car?

"Wait," Simone called out.

April stopped and raised her arms in confusion.

"What about traffic?" Simone asked.

It was all she could think of to prevent them from deciding to rent a car. Simone couldn't get in a car. There was no way. It terrified her to her core.

"What about it?" Lincoln asked.

"It gets bad. Very, very bad," Simone said. And it was true. She wasn't making it up. "We have to keep moving, right?"

April returned to the other two. "What the hell?"

"How far of a drive is it?" Simone asked.

"About forty-five kilometers," April said, "So we better stop twiddling our thumbs and hit the damn road."

"Wait a minute," Lincoln said as he let the thought digest. "Simone's right. The Palm is on the water. If we go by boat, we could potentially cut our travel time in half."

April shifted her gaze between the two. A conflict gleamed in her eyes.

"And we'll be a lot harder to follow if..." Simone let the thought trail. April and Lincoln both knew what she meant.

"Fine," April said. The edge on the word told Simone she was only compromising to save time.

The trio grabbed their bags and set off into the city of Dubai.

"It's some kind of scroll," Simone said as they walked into the modern desert metropolis. "Apparently, it leads to the location of the Fallen Star. Prince Kamal came here to sell it."

"Should I mention how we're following the lead of a man who tried to shoot us?" Lincoln said.

April quickened her stride. Simone could almost feel the heated anger burning off her skin.

Shortly, the trio came to a stop on the Dubai Metro. They collectively set their bags down.

"This should take us near the marina," Simone said.

"Have you been here before?" Lincoln asked.

Simone shook her head. "I researched it while you were asleep."

"Right," he said as it clicked in his head. "Insomnia." He studied her eyes with a skeptical glance. "You're not going to pass out from exhaustion on us, are you?"

"I wish," Simone said half-jokingly. If that's what it took to get some decent sleep, she'd almost take it. "When I'm awake, I'm awake."

The train arrived and took them within a block of the Dubai Marina.

The long stretch of water held a dozen or more docks, flanked by some of the tallest buildings Simone had ever seen. The lights of the city gave them an almost science-fictional look.

To Simone, being in a city was already an alien experience. Being dropped into the heart of one of the most opulent and rapidly expanding places on the globe had her feeling queasy. Or was that the hangover?

No, it was the field of skyscrapers jutting up from the sand, their shimmering steel and spotless glass, built on blood and oil. She wondered about the true cost of the desert paradise.

Shaking the thought from her head, Simone concentrated on the moment. They had to get the scroll. There wasn't time to ruminate on the philosophy of -

"Simone," Lincoln called.

She spun to face him.

He jerked his head in the direction of a thirty-three foot long sport fishing boat. "Let's go."

Simone stepped on board, feeling the vessel shift in the water. "Fishing?" she asked.

Lincoln shrugged. "Cheapest one they've got, but it's quick."

"An alibi helps, too," April added with her eyes cast toward the water.

The only other person on board was the captain who would pilot the boat. He lit a cigarette and pulled his sunglasses down from his head. "Where to?" he said and took a drag. "I can offer suggestions if you'd prefer. I know all the best spots. If you want the best fish, you've come to the right place."

"I want to see the Palm," Simone said. "Can you take us up close?"

The captain scrunched up his face. "There's no good fishing there. Why don't I take you to a spot I know? You'll get more than your money's worth."

"She said the Palm," April added. "Then we'll go fishing."

With a shrug and an exhale of smoke, the captain shrugged. "Whatever you say."

The captain guided the boat out of the marina as Simone rehydrated with a complimentary bottle of water and some fresh fruit.

Lincoln sat beside her.

"What's your plan?" he asked.

"Isn't that why you're here?"

"That's why we're all here. You spoke with the guy in the hospital. I thought you had something figured out and might want to share."

Simone took another sip of water. "I know what you know. I wouldn't keep something from you, if that's what you're wondering."

"That's not what I'm wondering."

"Then stop acting like it," she said.

Lincoln scratched his freshly shorn face. Even on the move, he still found the time to keep himself militarily proper.

"Maybe don't run off next time without letting us know where you are or what you're doing," he said. "You talk to me about being included and then do this kind of thing? What's up with that?"

Simone stared off, realizing that what he said was true. "I went out for fresh air. I had to clear my head. I just found myself looking for the guy. I didn't mean to, but that's what happened." She looked to Lincoln. "And at least when I do it, it doesn't end with shooting or torture. I'm not dragging you into a snake pit."

"What's that supposed to mean?"

"It means we're too different, you and I," Simone said, keeping her voice at a natural speaking level as to not upset the captain should he come within earshot. "You're the military gung-ho type, charging into battle, guns blazing. That's not me. At all. This…" She gestured all around. "Arms dealers and assassins in the night, breaking into catacombs…"

She let the thought hang and slowly exhaled.

Leaning forward, she added, "You don't need me. You need a *soldier*."

"Cut it out, Simone," he said, sounding disappointed.

"No, I'm not cutting it out," she said with agitation rising. "This may not be a big deal to you, but it scares the hell out of me, okay? Have you realized that yet? I'm scared to death, man."

Simone leaned back in her seat, too worked up to eat another bite.

Lincoln threaded his fingers together. "That's why we're here, Simone. To help and protect you. To make sure nothing happens."

"When this is over, I'm done," Simone said, looking Lincoln dead in the eye. "After the Fallen Star is found, that's it."

"Simone-"

"And don't try to talk me out of it."

"Your mind's really made up?" he asked.

Baffled, Simone shook her head, mouth agape. "Don't you think I've been considering this? What do you think I'm doing when I'm up all night? Looking at train routes? Yeah, I made up my mind. There's a lot of other things I'd rather be doing right now than stealing a scroll from a Saudi prince in Dubai, believe it or not."

Lincoln clapped his hands with finality. "So, that's it? You're just going to leave these antiquities sitting out there, waiting for guys like Prince Kamal and Felix Enderhoff to find them?"

Simone couldn't help but laugh at the thought.

Before she had a chance to think of a reply, the captain called back to them. "We are here."

Simone and Lincoln stood to get a view of the artificial island.

One feature dominated the outer center of the wide circle of land. A hotel - Atlantis The Palm - two towering structures linked by a central arching bridge. The massive, luxurious building cut an imposing figure against the seascape.

"Wow," April said as she joined the others.

"He's staying *here*?" Lincoln asked.

Simone nodded slowly, in awe of the sheer magnificence of the fantasy paradise. Even after their short trip through the city proper, Simone couldn't fathom how much wealth had been spent in this one dusty little corner of the world.

"We can't stop here," the captain called. "We must keep moving."

"Change of plans," Lincoln said.

The captain gave them a blank stare.

"Take us to shore," Simone said. "We have to make a quick stop."

"To shore?" The captain gave a shake of his head. "This is not a traditional request."

"Just do it," April said. "We'll be quick."

"Ooookay," the captain said, stretching the word out to indicate his apprehension.

Simone turned to Lincoln. "I feel under-dressed."

Lincoln nodded his agreement. All three of them were "dressed down", wearing gear one would wear trekking through the desert, not strolling through the polished marble lobby of an award-winning high-end hotel.

"What did you pack?" he asked.

Thinking, Simone shrugged. "What I always wear. This, sleeping stuff, like shorts, a tank."

"Let's just go," April said. "We'll be taking a break from a work trip."

"Working where?" Lincoln asked.

April made a wide gesture in the direction of the city. "Look around. Almost every building has a construction crane. This place is blowing up all over. Nobody's going to ask where we're working."

"Fair enough."

After the captain pulled into the nearest port, Simone, Lincoln, and April stepped off the boat and headed in the direction of Atlantis The Palm.

* * *

Simone stepped into the lobby and the hairs on her arms stood on end.

In the wide, circular space, a collection of massive stone pillars cut to resemble palm trees stood at the center of the awe-inspiring setting.

The polished floor beneath her boots was cleaner and more reflective than any surface Simone had ever seen. She almost didn't want to walk across it.

Lincoln gave April a knowing look. "Are you thinking what I'm thinking?"

April cracked a devious smile. "I'm thinking what you're thinking."

Totally in the dark, Simone followed Lincoln and April toward the check-in counter. En route, April broke off. Simone kept pace with Lincoln.

"Hi," he said to the friendly woman at the counter. "We have a package for Prince Orimer Kamal. A special request."

The woman flashed a white smile. "Of course. Just leave it here at the desk and I'll have it brought to his room right away."

"It's a rather large package," he added. "Is there any way we could-"

"Excuse me," April said as she rushed in, her face filled with worry. "Someone's sick over there." She pointed. "He's throwing up all over the place. It's really bad. It's *everywhere!*"

"Oh, my!" The woman's expression turned horrified as she rushed away from the counter. "I'll be right back!"

The small scattering of people in the lobby tracked the darting woman as she fled across the lobby in haste, leaving Simone, Lincoln, and April alone at the counter.

April poked her head around at the computer. "Got it," she said, turning to the others. "Neptune suite."

Lincoln nodded, looking from April to Simone. "Let's go find our Prince."

As they crossed the lobby, Simone asked, "Why didn't we just give her a real package and then follow it to the room?"

The trio stopped at the mouth of a hallway.

"Our method works, too," April said.

Lincoln pulled up a photo on his phone. "Here," he said, showing the image to the others. "This is our guy."

The image showed Prince Orimer Kamal in Washington, D.C. shaking hands with what Simone assumed were American political figures who didn't make the spotlight enough to be well-known. Weapons deals never made the top story, she thought.

"I'll stay back in case he checks out," Lincoln said. "I'll call if I see him leaving the hotel. Sound good?"

April nodded.

"Sounds good to me," Simone said.

"Be quick and be safe," Lincoln said before returning to the lobby.

Simone met eyes with April, who showed no animosity. When it was time to work, she worked and forgot everything else. Strictly business.

"It's down this hall," April said and started walking.

Simone followed. "Are you armed?" She figured the question was benign enough given the circumstances.

April shot a glance over her shoulder to Simone. "I'm always armed."

"April, this is a Saudi prince. If we shoot royalty, we're as good as dead."

Simone didn't know what kind of reasoning, if any, could get through to April, but she assumed April wasn't hot-headed enough to pull the trigger on a man so connected and important.

"I won't," April said. "And there's no such thing as royalty."

"What?"

"Royalty," April said. "It's make-believe. Nobody is special just because their pillaging murderer ancestors said so. That's a bunch of shit."

Simone never thought of it that way, but apparently April had strong feelings about it.

Ahead, a clutch of bodyguards turned the corner, followed by the dignitaries they were protecting.

Simone's heart skipped a beat when she saw him.

Prince Orimer Kamal, strolling down the hall, coming straight toward her and April.

"Act cool," April said in a low voice.

Then her tone of voice changed completely, becoming more relaxed and conversational. "Then he said we're meeting tonight at seven, so we should try to finish up by five-thirty so there's enough time to get ready…"

She trailed off as the group passed and continued on their way, paying the two women no mind. They had more important business to take care of.

April pulled Simone around a bend in the hallway and her voice lowered again. "Get to the room. Neptune Suite. I'll follow him in case he's going to make the deal."

"Okay," Simone said, although she wasn't entirely confident after seeing the well-protected prince in person. "I'll scope it out."

"Call the second you find the scroll," April said. She nodded, then peeled around the bend and followed after the prince's crowd.

Left by herself in the hallway, Simone psyched herself up with a deep breath and continued in search of the Neptune Suite.

13.

Dubai, United Arab Emirates

The door, as she expected, was locked.

Simone's eyes darted down both ends of the hall. There was nobody in sight. She could try to break down the door, but surely someone would hear that. She didn't know how to pick a lock, and besides, this was one of those electronic locks that required a key card. There was no way to pick it traditionally.

Everything in the hotel was state-of-the-art, Simone realized. It had to be, to attract royal clientele. It all had to be fresh, new, and clean.

Not just clean, but *spotless*.

Simone turned away from the locked door of the Neptune Suite and continued down the hall, moving along as if she was busy and couldn't be bothered. Hopefully the look would dissuade passersby from asking who she was and what she was doing.

She had no alibi if anyone did ask. She couldn't tell the truth - that she was on the lookout for the cleaning service to hopefully swipe a master key card from their cleaning cart.

As she walked, she pondered what her secret agent persona, Miss Rosa Munroe, would do. Simone had bluffed her way into Ahmed's hospital room, and the information she gathered all checked out.

Now that she was in Dubai, she needed the scroll that contained the location of the Fallen Star. In order to get that, she had to blend in.

Simone slipped through a door that led into an area of the hotel off-limits to the general public. The drab grey of the walls and exposed ducts stood in stark contrast to the display of opulence the public was exposed to. Further down the hall, she found a utility closet. All she needed was a uniform -

"Hey!"

Simone spun at the voice.

A short man approached. He wore a dark suit and an angry expression. He carried a walkie-talkie in one hand.

"Who are you?" he asked. "What are you doing back here?"

"Um," Simone said, buying a second to think. "I'm new. I was told to get a uniform."

"You're the new girl?"

She nodded.

The short man looked her up and down with skeptical eyes. "I didn't expect you to be so tall."

Simone shrugged. "I get that a lot."

"Stay here," the short man said. "I'll get you a uniform."

Simone breathed a sigh of relief once the man was gone. Now she just needed to bluff him enough to keep up the charade.

The short man returned with a gold-colored uniform draped over one arm. He lifted it for Simone to take. "Here."

"Thanks," Simone said, and took the uniform. She held it up to herself as a measurement. "It should fit just fine. I'll go try it on."

She left before he could say another word. She didn't look back.

In the public restroom, Simone pulled the pants over what she was already wearing and slipped into the light-colored button-up coat.

She stood before the mirror, inspecting her look.

"I guess I'm a Butler," she said to nobody.

An elderly woman approached where Simone stood in front of the mirror. "And you make a lovely Butler!"

Caught off guard, Simone simply smiled at the woman and left the restroom.

Simone patrolled the hallway in search of a key card to borrow. She assumed her traditional hairstyle of two braids was sufficient enough to maintain the illusion of her Butler disguise, given that nobody paid her any mind as they passed. Several individuals smiled or exchanged a friendly bow, but nobody seemed to notice that she wasn't really a Butler.

Turning another corner, Simone found a guest room door propped open by a cleaning cart.

Success.

She approached as if it was her own and looked for a key card. Nothing. She stepped in for a closer inspection.

"Excuse me."

Simone looked up, her breath catching in the back of her throat. She locked eyes with the woman cleaning the room.

"I'm sorry," Simone said. "My card isn't working, and I have to get into the Neptune Suite."

"Are you new?" the cleaning woman asked.

Simone nodded. "I just started about five minutes ago. I went to find the man who gave me the card, but he's gone, and I'm told the guest in the Neptune Suite needs something right away. I guess he's important?"

"That's Prince Kamal's room," the cleaning lady said. "Here, take mine." She tossed the key card to Simone, who snatched it out of the air.

"Thanks," Simone said. "I'll bring it right back."

She turned away.

"Hey," the cleaning said.

Simone froze.

"What's your name?"

Simone considered what to say. She didn't want to use her real name in case Prince Kamal found out someone had broken into his hotel suite.

"I'm Rosa," Simone said. "Rosa Munroe."

"I'm Claire," the cleaning woman said.

Simone smiled a friendly smile. "I'll be right back."

She hurried down the hall as quickly as she could without making it look like she was in a hurry. She hoped anyone who saw her would think she was just a Butler doing her job.

At the door for the Neptune Suite, Simone slid the key card into the slot. The door chimed in recognition as it unlocked. Simone pushed it open and slipped inside.

Letting the door close behind her, Simone gazed down at the staircase before her. She hadn't realized the suite spanned three floors of the hotel, but there she stood gazing down at the open area beyond the spiral staircase.

One wall was entirely glass and submerged in the surrounding water outside, like a giant aquarium. It was even filled with aquatic life, so much that Simone couldn't have counted all the fish swimming by if she tried.

"Wow," she said, her mouth agape at the sight.

She reached the lower section of the suite and found the bedroom. Naturally, she expected the most breathtaking view - that of the aquarium wall - to be found in the area where the guest would spend the most time.

She searched the bedside table, the dresser drawers, everywhere she thought might hold a valuable old piece of parchment.

She moved into another room on the lower floor, a living room of sorts. A common area for relaxation. It was there, on the centermost table, she saw the scroll.

It was left out as if it wasn't special at all, like it wasn't valuable enough to be locked away. The only window on this level was the glass aquarium wall, so the only prying eyes that would ever know it was there belonged to the fish.

Simone dropped to her knees at the table and studied the ancient scroll.

It was left unrolled, as if another party had been there doing the same - studying it, trying to uncover a hidden meaning.

The inscriptions were in a language Simone didn't recognize right away. Perhaps Greek?

This is why he wanted to sell the scroll, Simone thought. *He didn't want to go through the effort of deciphering the text.*

If Prince Kamal didn't care much about the Fallen Star, Simone wondered why he would be looking for it in the first place. Just to sell it? Why would a man of such wealth and prosperity go through so much trouble for more money? Surely there had to be easier ways...

Simone fished a hand into the pocket of the cargo pants that she wore under her Butler uniform and pulled out her cell phone. Instead of taking the scroll, she snapped a few photos - a wide shot and several closer images - just to make sure every part of it would be readable later.

She returned the phone to her pocket and rose to her feet. If she didn't get the key card back to Claire soon, she might start suspecting that something was wrong, that Rosa Munroe wasn't really a Butler at the Palm hotel.

Simone's heart stopped as she turned for the stairs.

A bodyguard, one she recognized from passing him in the hallway earlier with April, slowly descended the staircase.

"Nothing was requested for this room," the bodyguard said, suspicion strongly coloring his words. "Why are you here?"

Simone struggled to keep up the charade, sensing that this man already knew the truth.

"My boss told me to come down and check to make sure everything was in order. The last guest had a complaint, and we didn't want the Prince to experience anything but the best possible service." She forced an awkward smile.

The bodyguard nodded at the scroll on the table. "What are you doing with that?"

"I didn't know what it was," Simone said. "I assume it is Prince Kamal's."

"You assume correctly."

The bodyguard stepped off the last step and remained there on the floor so Simone could not leave.

"What was the complaint?" he asked. "That a Butler was sneaking into the suite and taking photos of personal belongings?"

Oh, crap...

"I'm sorry, I don't understand," Simone said, trying to play it off but knowing her cover was already blown.

"Show me your phone."

"I don't know what you mean," she said, inching her way away from the table.

The bodyguard's right arm reached behind his back and came around holding a monstrous handgun. He aimed it at Simone, never taking his eyes off her.

Simone froze in her tracks, hands rising in surrender.

"Please, let me explain."

"Can you explain why you're wearing boots?" he asked. "Is that the new Butler uniform?"

Simone's heart beat faster with each word spoken. She inched along, barely moving but doing her best to put the glass aquarium wall at her back. He wouldn't shoot and risk flooding the entire suite with himself in it.

It was a risk Simone was willing to take.

"Stop right there," he commanded.

With the glass wall now at her back, Simone stopped, her body positioned perfectly between the gun and the glass. "If you put the gun away, we can talk about this." In the extreme periphery of her vision, she noticed a faint glimmer of hope in the form of an elevator.

Of course a suite like this wouldn't force a high-paying guest to walk up the stairs.

She didn't know how she could lose him in an elevator when he could take the much quicker staircase, but it appeared to be the only way out.

The bodyguard made a call on his cell phone, still holding his aim on Simone. "You can discuss it with the Prince himself," he told her.

Simone found each new breath coming harder than the last. She was as good as dead if she didn't do something.

"Let me get my manager and he'll explain everything." Simone pointed to the door at the top of the staircase.

The bodyguard's arm shot out, fully extended with the gun barrel locked firmly on Simone. He didn't have to say a word. The message was delivered loud and clear - move again and die.

Her mind raced a mile a minute. The Prince would have her taken care of for sure. Once she was revealed as an American agent working for the United States government, all bets would be off. The country Prince Kamal was looking to sell to going behind his back to steal his information on the Fallen Star would all but cripple their working relationship.

Simone didn't know if that would be a good or bad thing, knowing the purpose of the weapons being traded - ongoing occupation in the Middle East, spreading "democracy" through destruction, creating refugees and furthering unrest, and all in the name of profit.

Her eyes darted back and forth as the bodyguard waited for his call to be answered on the other end. She had to remove herself from the equation, figuratively and literally.

But how? She saw no other way to escape. There could have been another door on her level in another room, but she couldn't risk darting off as long as the crosshairs were on her.

An idea sprang to mind.

Slowly, almost imperceptibly, she backed away from the staircase, easing herself closer to the aquarium wall and the small table that was pushed up against it.

"Prince Kamal," the bodyguard said into the phone.

Simone froze in place when she heard the conversation begin.

"Come down to the room," he said. "I have something you are going to want to see."

Simone reached behind her to grab whatever was on the desk. Her fingers fumbled with what felt like a marble statue roughly a foot tall, and heavy.

"I understand, your highness. I wouldn't have interrupted if it wasn't urgent."

She only had one chance to incapacitate the man. He stood roughly twenty feet from where Simone leaned against the desk. If she missed, she'd be shot. There wouldn't be a second chance.

"Yes, your highness. We'll be here awaiting your arrival."

The hang-up was her best chance, when he was momentarily distracted.

Heart racing in her chest, Simone breathed steadily, waiting for the bodyguard to return the phone to his pocket.

The call ended.

"He's on his way," the bodyguard said.

He lowered the phone and slipped it into his pocket.

Simone reacted as fast as she could. The marble statue came around and left her hand before the bodyguard even knew what had happened.

Simone raced after the statue as it hurtled toward the unsuspecting gunman.

He looked up one second before impact.

Lurching away from the heavy object, he ducked his head, raising his empty hand to protect himself.

Simone hoped and prayed the impact would knock him to the floor. She would leap over his body and be out of the room in a flash.

The statue struck the man in the head with a sickening thud.

A guttural grunt. The man fell sideways into the railing.

Simone slipped to one side of his slumping body. She was home free.

Then she heard the shot.

The gun discharged in the small area with a cataclysmic boom. Simone stopped on a dime, swinging around as a second sound followed.

The sound of glass spiderwebbing.

It first looked as if the wall was thick enough, reinforced well enough. But the spreading cracks in the glass betrayed that assumption.

She watched as the glass aquarium wall splintered, buckled, and gave way. The corner where the bullet struck exploded into tiny fragments.

The onrushing wave overcame the fractured glass and every drop of water from the other side spilled in with impossible speed.

Simone grabbed the groggy bodyguard by the arm and pulled him up the stairs, desperate for them both to escape the flood.

They made it up one step before the wave struck them down.

Water engulfed the room. Simone found herself lost in the tumbling torrent throwing her around effortlessly. She had no idea which direction was up.

Opening her eyes, she found she couldn't see through the foam of the surging tide.

Short on breath, Simone groped for the stair railing but her fingers grasped only water. And it continued to spill in from overhead.

There was too much.

Simone kicked her legs to try swimming through it all, but a sharp pain shot up her leg from her calf. She looked down and saw blood in the water. A lot of it.

Glass, she knew. Grabbing her calf, she felt the severity of the laceration. Simone then did the last thing she ever wanted to do in the kind of situation she was in.

She panicked.

Knowing she couldn't hold her breath much longer, knowing she needed to stop the bleeding right away, she looked everywhere for a way out of the flooded room.

Furniture tumbled through the rushing water. The fish and aquatic life that once lived beyond the glass wall now invaded the hotel suite.

Her lungs burned. She needed air.

Her foot touched bottom. Floor or ceiling? She couldn't tell. The entire room had flooded.

Looking ahead, she saw what looked like an unbroken section of the glass wall.

Simone made a desperate swim for it, powering through the pain in her leg, ignoring the tightness in her chest. Blood streamed behind her in frightening amounts.

Her world darkened. She found herself light-headed. Stars bloomed at the edge of her vision.

Simone was almost there. Almost within reach of the wall. Swimming through the break was her only chance to survive.

She couldn't hold her breath any longer. Her lungs felt on fire. But she was too far away to breathe just yet.

Too far.

Simone wasn't one to give up, but she knew her limits, and she knew she couldn't swim the whole way.

With a whimper, Simone's body took over, coughing out of sheer reflex as her mouth opened to find a life-saving breath.

Water filled her throat instantly. Gagging, she kicked and swam and pleaded and cried.

Simone's fingertips brushed the glass wall. She pushed off the bottom with her feet, clawing and scratching desperately against the glass to pull herself up for air.

Another cough and she found herself stopping, gagging on the water filling her lungs. She was almost to safety, but no matter how hard she swam, she made it no further.

Looking up, she saw tranquil shafts of sunlight wavering in the water's surface above.

Alone and sinking downward, a shrill series of screams left her mouth but were lost as soon as they were uttered, transforming into mute bubbles.

The heavy water darkened around Simone. Her limbs grew weary from frantic windmilling.

Slowly, her eyes closed, and the gagging on water filling her burning lungs stopped with one final sputter.

The panic she felt passed, and a sense of peace settled in, taking over each of her senses and wrapping her in a tranquility that eased her struggling.

Darkness enveloped her, and then all was still.

14.

Dubai, United Arab Emirates

Lincoln looked up suddenly, thrown on high alert at the sound coming from deeper within the hotel.

It sounded like a gunshot.

After that, a terrifying crashing of glass, water rushing within a tight space, too much water moving too fast, displacing everything in its path.

Commotion filled the lobby. Workers scrambled, many rushing toward the source of the sound, others hanging back and speaking in frantic whispers on their walkie-talkies, everyone desperate to know the source and cause of the colossal noise.

Lincoln eased away from where he stood, falling in behind the workers funneling down the hallway in the direction of the Neptune Suite.

He stopped suddenly, realizing only just then where Simone and April were last seen - heading in the same direction.

Scouring his pockets for his phone, Lincoln found it and hit the speed dial for Simone's cell.

He heard a ringtone, but nobody answered. An eternity passed before the voicemail message was heard.

"Shit!"

Thinking fast, Lincoln called April.

"What was that?" April said, bypassing any formalities of conversation.

"April, where are you? Get to the lobby as soon as you can."

"On my way."

April must have picked up on the stress in Lincoln's voice because she didn't say another word. She hung up and was standing next to Lincoln before the minute was up.

Huffing for breath, April looked toward the commotion that filled the lobby with the hallway to the Neptune Suite at the center of it all.

"Where's Simone?" she asked.

Lincoln stared at her, and slowly her eyes grew wider until her expression was fully replaced by a mask of sheer dread.

Looking toward the choked hallway, Lincoln knew there was no way through no matter what card they played. The only option was to go around and hope there was another route.

"Come on," he said and ran for the main rear doors of the lobby.

In the courtyard outside, Lincoln turned immediately in the direction of the Neptune Suite, never stopping until he found the source of the chaos.

The Ambassador Lagoon, a three-million-gallon open-air aquarium. To Lincoln's eyes the water level had dropped by several feet. The Neptune Suite had a glass wall that looked into the aquarium, but the bulk of that massive glass wall was missing, and the entire suite had been flooded.

The marine life within the aquarium scattered, unsure of what had happened, where to go to be safe, what to do next - much like the majority of onlookers who witnessed the aquarium wall's collapse.

Lincoln's eyes scanned one end of the water to the other but found no trace of Simone.

"Maybe she got out," he said, yet there was not a trace of optimism in his words.

No sooner was the statement uttered before April shouted, "There!"

Lincoln didn't have a chance to see. April dove into the aquarium without a second's thought. As she swam, the form came into Lincoln's view.

A lifeless form.

It was a woman's body, wearing a Butler's uniform. But Simone wasn't wearing a Butler's uniform. The thought brought some hope to Lincoln, but his heart sank when he saw the figure's black hair tied into two long braids.

She wasn't moving. Wasn't holding her breath. How long she'd been underwater, he didn't know, but the cloud of crimson pooling around her lower legs made Lincoln's limbs go numb at the sight.

He thought he saw sharks in the water. The sheer quantity of marine life in the aquarium was staggering, but it was all moving too quickly, scattering aimlessly as April pulled Simone's limp and unmoving body to the surface.

Lincoln reached over and pulled Simone from the water. Her dead weight was waterlogged, making it difficult for one man to move her, but adrenaline pumped through Lincoln's veins like never before.

He laid her down on the walkway and checked for vital signs.

"Simone, are you with me?" he said with a panic barely subdued.

April climbed out of the aquarium and went straight to work on Simone's leg, applying pressure to the wound.

"I need help!" she shouted to the nearest bystander. "Give me your belt!"

The startled tourist agreed, slipping the belt from his shorts and handing it to the soaking-wet tattooed stranger.

Lincoln felt no pulse, and Simone wasn't breathing. He tore open the Butler's uniform and began administering CPR.

April tied the belt around Simone's calf and shouted for a first aid kit.

Lincoln paid no attention to what was going on around him. He had to focus solely on Simone. After thirty quick chest compressions, he lifted her chin, tilted her head back, and gave two rescue breaths, watching to make sure her chest was rising and falling.

Thirty more compressions, then two more breaths.

Lincoln repeated the process over and over, not stopping for one second, not pausing no matter what. Thirty compressions and two breaths.

Thirty compressions and two breaths.

The crowd of onlookers grew, and hotel personnel pushed to the front. April held them back, nobody daring to challenge her fire and fury temperament.

Twenty-six compressions later and Simone coughed up water.

Lincoln felt a new surge of adrenaline hit as if he was the one who had been revived. He tilted her gently to the side so she wouldn't choke on the water coming up.

April jumped in, helping Lincoln hold Simone as she coughed up a startling amount of aquarium water.

Gasping for breath, Simone fell back into the arms of April and Lincoln. Her eyelids fluttered on the edge of consciousness.

"An ambulance is almost here," someone from the crowd said to April.

Lincoln brushed his fingers against Simone's cheek. "Simone? Simone, are you with us?"

Slowly, she opened her eyes and fixed Lincoln with a glassy stare. "Lincoln … How did you get here?"

"Simone, you drowned," Lincoln said.

Laughing in spite of the moment as an overwhelming feeling of thankfulness came over him, Lincoln wrapped his arms around Simone, hugging her as closely but as gently as he could.

"You lost a ton of blood," April said. "There's an ambulance on the way."

"Ambulance?" Simone seemed not to understand.

"You were dead for, like, minutes," April said. "You have to go to a hospital."

Simone turned to April as confusion gave way to comprehension. "Dead?"

"He brought you back." April pointed to Lincoln.

Simone looked to them both in turn, then shook her head, blinking her eyes and raising her hands to brush wet hair from her face.

"The glass wall in the Neptune Suite collapsed while you were inside," Lincoln said as the sound of emergency sirens approached.

"You're still bleeding," April said, holding her hands against the wound on Simone's leg. Blood seeped between her fingers. Her hands were stained red with Simone's blood.

Simone flinched as pressure was applied to the wound. Her body wasn't fully awake yet.

"Just sit tight," Lincoln said. "The ambulance is here."

"Ambulance…" Simone said groggily. "I can't…"

"Can't what?"

"I can't go in the ambulance." Simone pushed herself up to a seated position, but Lincoln held her by the shoulders, urging her to lie back.

A hotel employee stepped forward. "The ambulance has parked. They are on their way."

"No," Simone said. "I can't go."

Lincoln held her by the shoulders still. "Simone, just relax. It's going to be okay."

"I can't…" Simone struggled against Lincoln's grip but she was too weak. Her eyelids fluttered once more and she dropped back into his arms.

He checked her pulse at her neck and her wrist, just to be sure. She was still alive. Her chest rose and fell with soft breaths.

The medics pushed through the crowd. Lincoln greeted them.

"Is she okay? What happened?" one of them said.

"She was speaking a minute ago," Lincoln said. "She didn't want to go in the ambulance."

"Well, she has no choice," said another medic. This one attended to the wound on Simone's leg - a large, deep gash across her calf that was still bleeding.

Lincoln and April rose to their feet and stepped away for the medical professionals to take care of Simone.

Leaning closer to Lincoln, April said, "Why didn't she want to go in the ambulance?"

* * *

Simone opened her eyes to the somber, electronic dirge of medical monitoring equipment at her bedside.

Blinking, she tried to sit up but could hardly even raise her arms to push herself up. Every muscle in her body felt brand new, as if they had never been used before. Her head felt as if it weighed nothing. Then when she tried to turn it to one side, it felt as if her head weighed a hundred pounds.

Her senses were all muddy, functioning like a computer that could turn on but not boot all the way. Something inside her had been reset.

She remembered water. A lot of it. It surrounded her, enveloping her in its cold fingers. She remembered glass shattering.

She remembered the crushing wave.

A shuddering breath escaped, and her heart beat more heavily.

"Simone," said the voice of Lincoln. "She's awake," he called to someone else.

Simone found Lincoln sitting by her bedside. April hurried in from the hallway.

"Where am I?" Simone asked in a parched voice.

"In the hospital. In Dubai," Lincoln said. "Do you remember?"

Simone nodded as best as she could, which wasn't much. Just enough for Lincoln to understand that she did, in fact, remember.

"My phone," Simone said before coughing. Her lungs ached as if they had been beaten. It hurt to catch her breath.

"We have all your things," April said. "Your phone is with them, all your clothes, your boots, whatever you were wearing."

Only then did Simone realize she was wearing nothing but a hospital gown under the blankets that were pulled up to her shoulders.

"My phone," she repeated.

Lincoln turned to April. "Get the phone."

"It's waterlogged," April said with a shrug, as if asking if it'd even work.

"Get it anyway." Lincoln turned back to Simone. "Just rest. You don't have to say anything."

Simone managed to raise her hands and bring them to her face. She rubbed her sleepy eyes with fingers that felt like jelly. No part of her seemed to work right. Even her mind was foggy and confused. She felt incomplete.

"Cursed," she said to herself.

"Don't even start with that," Lincoln said.

She turned her head to face him. "I really…?" She left the sentence unfinished, afraid to say the word.

"Yes," Lincoln said, his voice taking on a solemn tone.

"Wow," Simone said. "I was really dead? Like, clinically dead?"

He nodded. "You don't remember?"

"I remember the wall coming down," she said. "The water rushed in and that was it. Next thing-" She coughed a dry cough again. "Next thing I remember, I'm outside looking up at you."

There seemed to be no period of transition in Simone's mind. One second, she was watching the aquarium wall shatter, the next, she was awaking from the deepest sleep she'd ever experienced. She'd seen no white light, no angelic figures, felt no passage to the other side. Nothing like it was in the movies.

That scared her more than the fact that she actually drowned.

April returned with Simone's phone. "It was a bitch to get this," she said and handed it to Lincoln. She turned to Simone. "Police want to speak to you when you're awake. I didn't tell them you were."

"Thanks," Simone said.

The raspy, dry quality of her throat made it difficult to speak. Lincoln helped her with a glass of water. She got down a few sips, but didn't feel like any more.

"What's on the phone?" Lincoln said, holding up the little device for Simone to see.

"Greek," she said.

"Greek?"

Simone nodded a slight nod. "Pictures of the scroll. I thought-" She worked through another coughing fit. "I thought it would be smarter than taking it."

"So he wouldn't wonder where it disappeared to," Lincoln said with a grin. "Smart thinking."

"I was hoping we could decipher it and beat him there," Simone said and motioned for more water.

Lincoln held the glass and tipped it toward Simone's lips for her to sip. "Well, it was a good idea at the time. I guess we just have to hope that the scroll was lost in the water."

Simone waved the glass away, shaking her head. "No." She swallowed. "We can still do it."

April stepped forward. "You're in a hospital, Simone. An hour ago, you were *dead*. You're not going anywhere."

Simone exhaled. Part of her felt defeat. Another part felt that she could prove April wrong.

Turning to Lincoln, she said, "How long will it take to decipher it?"

Lincoln shook his head. "If we can even get the phone to work. Are the photos in the cloud, or just here?"

Simone raised a feeble hand and pointed to the phone.

All optimism faded from Lincoln's expression. "We'll get to work on it."

"I'll see if I can get some rice from a market or somewhere," April said. She started for the door. "Wish me luck."

Simone relaxed back on the pillow, staring up at the ceiling.

She found it impossible to rest. Not because of a dream this time, but because she hated being tied down, confined to a bed and unable to do anything.

Minute by minute, she felt better. The fog in her head was mostly clear, and her limbs felt more like they belonged to her once again. Before, it was as if she was a puppeteer manipulating the soft and clumsy arms of a marionette.

Thinking back on the events that transpired in the Neptune Suite, it all felt like a dream rather than something which actually occurred.

Dead, she thought, laughing to herself.

"What is it?" Lincoln asked.

"Do you know that nurse at the air force base? The one who gives the physical?"

"I have a male physician," he said. "But yes, I know who you mean. I think her name is Michaela."

Simone rolled her eyes sideways to look into Lincoln's. "She's going to have a stroke when she hears about this."

They shared a laugh together.

"But seriously," Simone said. "Don't tell her."

Lincoln held up his hands and leaned away. "Hey, that's all on you."

Simone figured she'd cross that bridge when she came to it. She had to focus on the Fallen Star, on getting out of the hospital. The longer she was held up in bed, the closer Prince Kamal would get.

She couldn't let that happen. Not after what she'd been through already.

She didn't want to have died for nothing.

15.

Dubai, United Arab Emirates

Prince Orimer Kamal ordered one of his servants to push aside the police tape that had been strung up in the hallway, preventing anyone from getting close enough to the Neptune Suite to see exactly what had happened.

The Prince stepped into the hall and proceeded to the door of the suite. It hung wide open. He thought at first about his belongings in the room, that anyone at all could easily sneak through the feeble police tape barrier and waltz into his room at any given moment.

Stepping closer to the doorway, he peered into the room.

There was water in the room. A lot of it. Hundreds of thousands of gallons. The entire first floor was submerged. The water level crested somewhere in the middle of the second floor. By the looks of it, the entire suite sustained water damage. This was the best the staff could do to pump the water out.

Prince Kamal's eyes burned with volcanic intensity. He didn't turn his head to look at his servants when he spoke. "What is the meaning of this?"

"We do not know yet, your highness. We are working to find out what happened." The servant hesitated. "One of your bodyguards was found dead in the water."

Still, Prince Kamal did not turn away from the flooded Neptune Suite.

The servant cleared his throat. "Another body was found, your highness. It was a woman. Witnesses say she was wearing the attire of a Butler, but when the attire was removed, she was wearing other clothes beneath."

Prince Kamal turned his head, his eyes locking on the servant. "She was in the room?"

"Yes, your highness."

"How did she get inside, if she is not actually a Butler?"

The servant lowered his head. "I do not know, your highness. She was taken away by ambulance."

Prince Kamal shifted himself around, facing the servant. "She survived?"

He nodded.

"Find her," Prince Kamal demanded. "And find the scroll. I don't care who you have to bribe. I want it in my hand before sundown this night."

"You will have the scroll, your highness," the servant said. "The translator will be arriving soon."

"Good," the Prince said. "Make sure he has something to translate. I cannot afford to look like a fool."

"Yes, your highness."

Two of the servants disappeared down the hallway. The two others lingered near the Prince, ready to carry out whatever order they would be given.

Prince Kamal stared again into the flooded suite.

Someone was on his tail. He didn't know who, he didn't know how, but he would find out. Whoever it was trying to get between him and Murad Abdullah would not live to see whether the Fallen Star possessed any magical healing powers or not.

Murad, the Prince thought. *He must be the one behind this.*

It had to be. Murad would steal the scroll, making Prince Kamal look even more incompetent, and he would hire a woman to do it to add insult to injury.

A string of curses flew from Prince Kamal's mouth. He'd be damned if Murad would have the last laugh and walk away with the scroll *and* the Star in the end, keeping all of the money promised in their agreement.

Prince Kamal faced his two servants. "Remain here and let no one through other than myself. If the resort management asks questions, say you were hired by the authorities to protect the Prince's valuables."

"Yes, your highness," they both said.

"If the authorities question you, alert me to their presence at once. Stall them as long as necessary."

The two servants bowed as Prince Kamal rushed off in a storm of billowing robes.

* * *

The plane touched down as the golden sun of a new day rose in the United Arab Emirates.

Solomon had with him only one carry-on bag. Lilly had set him up with a contact for acquiring weapons in Dubai. He never traveled with a weapon, not even a pocket knife, even though he could easily get away with it if he wanted to. There were ways around every screening procedure known to man, but taking the risk meant increasing the possibility of giving up the reward.

Once Lilly had informed him of a private flight to Dubai from Andrews AFB carrying three parties, he knew those three parties were Lincoln Lewis, April Farren, and the reward herself - Simone Winifred Cassidy.

Solomon stepped out of the airport and paused to light a cigarette and take in the beauty of the city's magnificent construction. He pulled his sunglasses down from his head and over his eyes as the hot sun beat down. He greatly preferred this warm climate to Norway's less forgiving chill.

The big news story, he found out on the flight over, was the collapse of an underwater hotel suite at the Palm resort. Nothing of the sort had ever happened before. Dubai was renowned for its construction. The event had suspicion written all over it. No better place to start looking.

But first, he needed a gun.

* * *

Solomon met with the man named Murad Abdullah at a beachfront restaurant with a magnificent view of the sandy beach.

Even though the restaurant was not yet open for business that early in the day, Solomon found Murad sitting with his back to the water and a bowl of fresh fruit before him.

"You must be Solomon." Murad rose to shake the stranger's hand.

"And you must be Murad."

Murad nodded and gestured for Solomon to sit while he lowered himself back down and continued eating berries and figs.

"We are okay to speak here?" Solomon asked.

"My cousin owns the restaurant," Murad said. "Nothing is off the table. You may speak and eat whatever you wish."

Solomon eyed the assortment of fruits. Half of them, he couldn't identify by name. This told him that the Murad fellow sitting at the other end of the table valued the exotic, perhaps more intrigued by simply having the uncommon than actually partaking of it, as his consuming of the more pedestrian fare indicated.

If there was a way to get on this man's good side, Solomon knew it was to appeal to the man's status rather than attempting to impose on what he took pride in.

"I just came for the weapons," Solomon said.

Murad wiped his hands clean with a napkin. "Getting straight to business, I see. Tell me, Solomon, what is it that you wish? Your contact was not thorough in explaining this to me."

"I like to keep things simple," Solomon said. "I'm looking for something close-quarters and something long-range. The target is always on the move."

Murad waved for Solomon to stop talking. "You don't need to explain anything to me, young man. The less I know, the better it is for all of us. I have what you need."

He signaled for a bodyguard to bring something to the table.

Solomon had not even seen the guard sitting across the dining area, cloaked in shadow. He wondered how many other bodyguards would be watching within earshot.

Murad moved the fruit bowl aside and the bodyguard brought a wooden crate to the table. He removed the lid and stepped away. Solomon had to stand to see inside.

Murad reached inside and came away with a handgun. "Caracal semi-automatic. This is what the police use. It is the most common handgun in Dubai." He handed it to Solomon.

Solomon held the weapon in his hand, feeling the weight. He ejected the magazine, slid it back in and rose to aim at the open sand, checking the sights.

"It comes in a smaller, more compact variation." Murad held up a variation of the pistol in Solomon's hand. "Government agents who need to conceal a firearm carry this. It might be preferred, depending on your needs."

"It just needs to work," Solomon said with no inflection. To him, it was just a job.

Murad reached into the crate and found another handgun. "In that case, you might be interested in this."

He pulled out a monster, something that reminded Solomon of the crazy bloodfest action movies he grew up watching where everything was jacked to the max, from the weapons to the muscles of the heroes blasting away with reckless abandon.

"Desert Eagle fifty caliber," said Murad. "For when you just need to kill something."

Solomon exchanged the Caracal for the Desert Eagle. Holding the weapon made him feel powerful, able to handle whatever was put in front of him.

Murad continued, "I have a cache of those outfitted with experimental ammunition. Armor-piercing rounds. Many of my enemies wear body armor. You have heard the news about the glass wall collapsing in in the Palm resort hotel?"

"I have."

Murad took the Desert Eagle from Solomon and held the weapon for him to see. "This is what did it, with my experimental ammunition. When I say not to doubt its power, remember that."

"I'm not sure I need something that intense. The Caracal will do fine."

"Very well," Murad said. "And for long-range? Are you firing across a field, or across the city?"

"Let's split the difference," Solomon said. "Standard issue sniper rifle."

Murad called for the bodyguard, who came and took away the crate of handguns. Another bodyguard brought a second crate and removed the lid.

Murad spread his arms before the assortment of state-of-the-art sniper rifles.

"Take your pick."

16.

Dubai, United Arab Emirates

Simone stood on her own for the first time in twenty-four hours.

Lincoln walked through the door to the hospital room just as she was making it back to her bed.

"Simone, what are you doing up? Did the nurse say you could get out of bed?"

Simone held one hand against the wall for balance as she walked. "When you've gotta go, you've gotta go, whether there's a nurse around or not."

Simone got back to the bed and paused with her palms resting on the side.

Lincoln stepped up to help.

"I got this," Simone said, and waved him off.

She took a breath and slowly climbed back into bed. Moving around didn't hurt at all. That wasn't the issue. It was that her limbs still felt wobbly and unsure. Her muscle memory seemed to be the last thing coming back to her.

"Should you be out of bed?" Lincoln asked again.

"I was out of bed and the world didn't end," Simone said. "I'm fine, for real. This bed is the only thing holding me back."

"How so?"

"I need to get up and move, Lincoln," she said. "This is the most I've sat still in … I don't even know how long."

She sighed, frustrated by the situation. An athlete confined to a hospital bed was akin to caging a hungry cheetah that needed to hunt. Simone was never more out of her element than when she was healing from injury.

And as strange as it seemed to her, she didn't consider dying to be the worst that had happened to her. She felt that if she could just get up, stretch her legs, and get moving once again, she would be as good as new in a few short days.

Changing the subject, she said, "Did you get the images from my phone?"

Lincoln sat in the chair beside the bed. "I'm almost afraid to say yes."

"Why?"

"Because I know as soon as I do, you're going to be putting your clothes on and telling me it's time to hit the road."

Simone perked up. "Tell me you've had it translated!"

Lincoln sighed. "It's been translated."

"What did it say? Do you know where the Fallen Star is?"

"I've got a pretty good idea."

"What does that mean?" Simone asked.

Lincoln rubbed his face. "It's being housed *in a lofty place*."

"What does *that* mean?"

He shook his head. "April has a theory."

"Lay it on me."

"The word used in the text is *meteora*. The language being Greek, we figure it's somewhere in Greece."

"At the Meteora monasteries," Simone said.

Lincoln studied her curiously.

"I read about them in college after I blew out my knee doing hurdles," Simone said. "It all makes sense."

"Humor me," Lincoln said.

"The monasteries were built in the fourteenth century, around the same time as the Black Death. If the Fallen Star is what we think it is…"

She paused as her thoughts went to the Serpent's Fang and how she doubted its powers. She wouldn't make that same mistake again.

"If it was used in some way to put an end to the plague," she continued, "then whoever was in possession would want to keep it somewhere secret and safe, where nobody else could reach it. A monastery on top of a giant rock formation with limited access would be the perfect spot."

Lincoln's expression changed from mild intrigue to utter captivation. "I think I'm sufficiently humored."

Simone swung her legs over the side of the bed and climbed down to the floor. "So, do you know what time it is?"

Lincoln gave a slow shake of his head. "Simone-"

"There's a road that needs hitting, and it leads to Greece."

She steadied herself with one hand on the bed as she turned to the closet where her clothes hung.

Lincoln got up and shuffled one step toward stopping Simone, but halted as she reached the closet, threw open the door, and took her clothes out.

Simone got the feeling that he knew better than to try to stop her. She had a knack for not backing down, and any form of injury only served to further convince her that she was more than capable of whatever task was put before her.

"Where's April?" Simone asked. "Is she already on her way there?"

"She's grabbing something to eat. Simone, you can't just leave."

With her clothes bundled in her arms, Simone turned to Lincoln. "Why not? I said I'm fine."

She ambled toward the bathroom, visibly not quite fine enough to go trekking through Greece or scaling a mountainous cliffside. But that didn't matter, because in her head, she knew she could do it.

"Because the police are still outside," Lincoln said.

Simone halted, clothes in one hand, bathroom door in the other. "I talked with them yesterday. What are they still doing here?"

"I don't know, but they have the front and back doors guarded. They're either trying to keep someone from getting in, or keep you from getting out."

Simone drew a long breath and exhaled through her nose. "We'll talk about this when I have clothes on."

With that, she swung the door shut for privacy.

Lincoln started to protest but stopped himself, realizing the futility of the attempt.

It took Simone three times as long as it normally would to dress herself. Her arms felt more normal than her legs, but she was using her arms more frequently, and that convinced her that her legs would feel as good as new once she got moving again. The worst part would be dealing with the gash in her calf, which required a large number of stitches. But that, too, would heal.

All she needed was time.

After swapping the hospital gown for her own clothes, Simone stood before the mirror. Her hair was a disaster, so she gave it a quick finger-combing and tied it into two braids.

Watching herself as she worked as quickly as her fingers would allow, she had a difficult time understanding exactly what had happened the day before, that it had happened to her. She expected the reality of the moment to come crushing down, but it hadn't. At least not yet.

Simone laced up her boots and stepped out of the bathroom as April was entering the room.

April looked her up and down as if someone was playing a joke on her that she didn't understand.

"What's this all about?" she asked, and turned to Lincoln. "Do you know about this?"

Lincoln simply shook his head in a gesture that made Simone feel like a child, that he was her legal guardian yet unable to dictate how she lived her life. She'd seen the look too many times in the past. She hadn't appreciated it then, and she didn't appreciate it now.

"What?" she asked Lincoln. "Don't we have a deadline?"

"Don't you remember what happened yesterday?" he asked in disbelief, his voice rising in volume with every word spoken. "This is insane."

"Yeah?" she said. "Well, it's what we're doing."

"So, you're just going to take over this mission?"

"It's what *I'm* doing," she said. "Are you going to join me or sit here and wait? Every minute that passes, the closer Prince Kamal gets to the Fallen Star. Do you want to let that happen?"

"I don't want to let you hurt yourself." Lincoln's voice softened as his argument shifted to emotional reasoning. "Remember last year, you told me you couldn't leave Saipan until your shoulder was healed? That you didn't work unless you were healthy enough? I remember."

Simone lowered her eyes.

Lincoln continued, "I remember you sat on that island for a month before we found you, and you still didn't want to leave. Now you literally rise from the dead and can't wait to get out and continue on as if nothing happened? I know you don't want to hear this, Simone, but you can't push yourself too hard."

A long silence followed Lincoln's statement.

April didn't move from where she stood except for her eyes shifting between the two parties, as if watching hunter and prey, not knowing what the next move was going to be.

Simone stared at the shiny hospital floor, at her dirty boots that felt strange after being waterlogged, as if her feet didn't belong in them.

Everything Lincoln said was true, Simone admitted to herself. Starting the journey was always the hardest part, working to convince herself that it was worth the effort. But once that journey began, Simone had no way of shutting off the desire to complete the task. Not even injury could stop the drive. Not even death.

She took a moment to compose her thoughts to voice as words.

"I also remember you telling me about trust." Simone raised her eyes to meet Lincoln's. "I know that I'm all right. I know that I'm not one-hundred-percent, but I know that I'm ready to move on to the next step, and when we get to the next step, I'll be ready for the one after that. I can do this. Whatever your perception is of me ... that isn't *me*, and it's not going to hold me back when I know what I can and can't do."

Another wave of silence sucked the air out of the room. Lincoln found himself looking to April for her opinion.

April held her hands up and backed away. "Hey, this is your beef. I've got nothing to do with it."

Lincoln turned to Simone and nodded in surrender. "Okay," he said. "Your call."

Simone traded a glance with April. "What's the best way out of here?"

April pointed, but Simone didn't know the layout of the facility at all. Front or rear, she didn't have any idea.

"Guards take their breaks in shifts," April said. "One goes, the other stays."

"Think we can sneak past one guard?" Lincoln asked.

"Easier than sneaking past two." April went for the door. "I'll call when it's break time."

Simone and Lincoln nodded, and April left the room, leaving the two of them standing there awkwardly. Simone didn't know what to say, so she stayed quiet.

She still felt uneasy on her feet, as if she was standing on a boat rocking in gentle waves. She breathed through it, centering herself, knowing that the sensation would pass.

"I'm sorry," Lincoln said, breaking the silence.

Simone sat on the edge of the bed to take some pressure off her stitched-up leg. "It's okay. I know you're just looking out for me," she said. "And I appreciate that."

"It's just that…" Lincoln found the words hard to get out. He took a deep breath. "I felt your wrist when there was no pulse. I felt your heart when it wasn't beating. I saw your lungs not filling with air. And that scared me."

He drew another breath and sat down, rubbing his hands together nervously. Only then did Simone see how someone other than her was affected by what had happened.

Clearly struggling to get his thoughts out, Lincoln said, "I never want to see that again."

In typical military tough-guy fashion, Lincoln kept his emotions close to the vest and maintained a controlled disposition at all times, but he couldn't hide what he was feeling just then. It showed on his face, in his wounded eyes, in the way he looked at Simone as if silently pleading that she not rush back into action and cause herself greater harm by doing so.

Simone lowered her head. She couldn't believe she didn't consider how he must have felt, being the one who actually brought her back from clinical death. She suddenly felt as if her entire outlook on the operation, her distrust of it all, had been so terribly wrong.

"Wow," she said in a low voice. "I'm kind of terrible, aren't I?"

"You're not terrible, Simone."

"I just never thought about…"

"It's fine," he said. "There's a lot going on, a lot to think about."

Simone sat quiet for a moment, wondering if she was indeed moving too quickly.

Before she could finish her thought, Lincoln's phone chimed.

He glanced at the screen, then looked up at Simone. "April says the guard is on break."

They locked eyes, and an unspoken understanding passed between them.

They both stood, and Simone followed Lincoln into the hall, leaving the door to her hospital room wide open.

"This way," Lincoln said, guiding Simone through the unfamiliar corridors.

She kept her head down and walked as quickly as she was able, which was just fast enough that Lincoln didn't have to stop for her to catch up.

They found April waiting at the mouth of a perpendicular hallway.

"Hurry up," she whisper-shouted as the duo approached. "The first one's gone to the cafeteria, so we don't have a lot of time."

"What's the plan?" Lincoln asked.

"Don't worry," April said. "I have an idea."

Simone narrowed her eyes at April. "Does this one involve people running around frantically like the last one?"

April put her hand on the fire alarm. She cracked a devious grin.

And pulled the fire alarm.

Instantly, the building was thrown into confusion. Flashing lights and blaring sirens resounded down every corridor. A calm but firm voice came over the public address, instructing everyone to exit the building in a safe and orderly manner.

The one police guard remaining at the exit jumped to his feet and darted down the hall, leaving the door completely unguarded.

April led the way out with Simone and Lincoln following close behind.

"What about our bags?" Simone said as she hurried away from the evacuating hospital.

"We've got a hotel." Lincoln pointed to the train station two hundred yards ahead. "Train will take us there."

Simone gave one quick glance over her shoulder at the chaos in and around the hospital, thankful to be out, yet wishing there was an easier way to continue. Disrupting an entire hospital just to leave?

She came to the realization that there were parts of the job she would never reconcile herself to.

* * *

Simone didn't see the inside of the hotel. She waited on a bench with April as Lincoln went in to retrieve their luggage so they could hop on a plane to Greece ASAP.

The vision of the panicked hospital stuck in Simone's head. She wiped sweat from her brow as the sun beat down.

She turned to April, wondering what to say. She couldn't just blurt out that her actions weren't the best option given their circumstances. Sometimes, a more covert approach was called for.

Simone lifted the leg of her cargo pants to inspect the stitches in her calf. All the jogging and walking had it feeling sore. She hoped she still had some painkillers in her bag.

April sat leaning forward with her arms resting on her knees and her fingers threaded together. She stared straight ahead without a word.

Simone wished she would help facilitate the conversation, but after a minute of nothing, Simone knew it fell on her.

"Lincoln told me you pulled me out of the water," Simone said. "I never said thanks."

"Don't mention it." April held her gaze forward.

The coldness of the reply left Simone wondering what she ever did wrong to upset April. Was she really still holding a grudge about what happened in Brno?

"Do you…" Simone started, wondering if she should even bother continuing. "Do you have a problem with me?"

April turned her head toward Simone. "Problem?"

"It's just a question." Simone shook her head slightly, regretting that she brought it up.

"You weren't called back so you could run the operation, you know."

"I do know," Simone said.

April snorted a brief laugh. "You haven't stopped making demands since you showed up. Then you question my decisions? Do you know how long I've been doing this?"

"No," Simone said in a low tone, hoping to avoid any more conflict between them.

"This is the job," April said. "We know what works. We know how it has to be done. I don't need a part-timer telling me how to do my job, all right?"

"All right, fine. I'm sorry I ever brought it up."

Lincoln stepped out into the bright sun with every-one's bags.

"We're all checked out. Our plane should be arriving in half an hour," he said, picking up on the weird vibe between the two women. "Is everything okay?"

"Yeah," April said as she stood and took her bag from Lincoln's arm.

He looked to Simone for help but she just shook her head.

Taking her bag from Lincoln, Simone searched it for the bottle of painkillers she had stashed away, not bothering to hide them anymore.

She spilled two into her hand and swallowed them dry.

Lincoln watched as she put them back.

Simone hefted her bag over her shoulder and their eyes met.

"For my leg," she said.

Not another word was exchanged among the group until they boarded the private plane thirty minutes later.

Simone sat away from the other two with her eyes closed. Before, she had harbored thoughts of this being her last mission with Clark's crew. As the flight took off, she had her mind made up conclusively.

She was never going to work for Clark again.

17.

Thessaly, Greece

The plane touched down at the tiniest private airfield Simone had ever seen.

Gazing out the window and through the dark of night, she could only barely make out countryside framed by surrounding mountains. At first, she didn't realize how late at night it was. With no light pollution, the stars shone bright and the half-moon acted as a dim sun.

Yawning, Simone gathered her things and exited the plane after April and Lincoln. The two of them had both slept like babies without stirring even once.

Simone was forced awake throughout the entire five and a half hour trip. She dozed off periodically only to be jolted awake by one vision or another. If it wasn't the deaths she caused in Mexico continuing to haunt her, it was the sight and sound of the glass aquarium wall from the Neptune Suite in Dubai crashing in around her.

She woke up gagging for breath on two different occasions. The feeling that she was still underwater, that she was unable to draw a breath, felt too real.

She had popped a couple more painkillers and rinsed them down with one of the small bottles of whiskey she'd taken from the previous flight that were still stashed away in her bag. After that was finished and she still couldn't find peaceful slumber, she searched quietly for more of those little bottles of booze, trying not to wake April or Lincoln. She found two more whiskeys and another gin. Into her bag they went.

All she had managed to do on the flight was get herself high and drunk. But at least her leg felt fine. By the time they landed, the effects had worn off and left her sleepier than she had been before.

Standing in the cool darkness on the landing strip, Simone shivered and yawned again, curious to know how they would get to the monasteries at Meteora.

Lincoln waved April and Simone toward where he stood. Once the trio was together, he answered Simone's unasked question for her.

"There's a stable a quarter-mile north, but we have to walk to get there," he said.

"Stable?" April asked. "As in, horses?"

"Yes, horses," he replied. "Can you ride a horse?"

Simone realized the question was directed specifically to her. "Oh, um … I rode a little when I was a kid."

"That's good enough. We should be able to reach the monasteries by sunrise."

"Then what?" April asked.

"Then we get inside and go from there. We can figure the rest out on the way." Lincoln nodded in the direction they had to go and started walking. April and Simone followed.

Long minutes passed and the only sound from either of the three was Simone's yawning.

"Didn't get much sleep?" Lincoln finally asked.

"I couldn't," Simone said. "My sleep schedule was messed up enough, but the hospital stay, like, reset everything. But I'll be fine. I just need to keep moving."

The more she walked over the uneven terrain, the more the wound on her leg felt sore. She wasn't sure what she'd feel like by the time they climbed all the way up to the monastery.

"I have an idea," she said. "If you'd like to hear."

"Shoot," Lincoln said.

"We need an alibi to get in, right? Then we're traveling on a pilgrimage. You're a priest," she said to Lincoln.

He chuckled. "Me, a priest?"

"And April and I are nuns accompanying you. I know, it's hilarious, but it could work. We have to stop because I fell along the way and I need to rest. I've got the gash to prove it. They won't ask questions when they see it."

"What about the stitches?" April asked.

"I don't know," Simone said, thinking. "I got them … somehow. Somewhere along the way."

"No, April's right," Lincoln said. "That's a professional job. They'll know as soon as they look."

Simone felt her strategy unraveling. "Then … then I'll rip them out."

April turned a glance to Simone, one of disbelief.

Lincoln scoffed. "That still won't work."

"Why not?"

"Because they'll see the marks in your skin where you were stitched. And I can't even believe we're discussing this."

Simone considered what Lincoln had said. He was right - they'd see where the skin was punctured.

"Wait," April said. "Forget the leg thing. One of us could just pretend to be sick."

Lincoln pointed to April. "I like it. Simple, easy to fake. Who's going to be ill?"

"Not me," said April, raising her arms to show her tattoos in the dim starlight. "Would a nun have these? I've gotta stay covered up."

"True," Lincoln said. He looked to Simone. "It's either you or me."

"I'll do it," she said. "I won't have to pretend to be tired by the time we get there, and we can still use the leg idea. Maybe I messed it up in Athens and had it stitched up there, but we continued on the pilgrimage anyway and now I have to rest."

The trio all traded a look, silently voting on the idea. Lincoln nodded, then April.

They continued walking in silence, and Simone yawned again as the ache in her leg intensified.

* * *

Dubai, United Arab Emirates

"They checked out?" Solomon asked.

The older woman behind the front desk nodded with a look of sadness on her face.

"Bummer," he said. "I was hoping to catch them before they left. Did they say why they left in such a hurry?"

"No, sir. The man checked them all out, all three."

Solomon sighed. One step behind once again.

"Would you like a room, sir?" the older woman asked.

Solomon shook his head. "I have to get going myself. Thank you for your help."

He dialed Lilly's number on his cell as he walked out of the hotel in the direction of the airport. Unlike his prey, this hunter did not have the luxury of private and immediate air travel.

Lilly answered, "What's up?"

"They left Dubai. Check flight logs."

"Destination?"

"Don't know," he said. "There's still a bit of daylight here. They might not have landed yet. Keep your eyes peeled."

"You got it, baby." Lilly snapped her gum. "This seems like an awful lot of work to track this girl down. Are you sure she's that important? You could always come back home and help me warm up the bed."

"Sorry, hon. The bed will have to be cool for another day or two."

Lilly made a *hmmf* sound of displeasure. "Promise me you won't take on any more business until we have a little vacation of our own. Have you been to Belize? I've always wanted to go."

"This isn't business," he said. "It's personal."

He came to a sudden halt in front of a cafe with a TV visible from the window.

"Hold on…"

He couldn't hear the audio, but he saw a news broadcast displaying images from the disaster at Atlantis The Palm. The resort appeared to be running as usual with one little section of the hotel cordoned off behind police tape and safety barricades.

There was nothing on the scrolling ticker at the bottom of the screen to indicate exactly what happened in any detail, but a new image appeared on the screen.

It looked to Solomon like a still frame from a security camera inside the hotel. A Butler stood in front of the door to the Neptune Suite. She was tall, with long, braided black hair.

Solomon stopped the nearest pedestrian. "Hey, where is this?" He pointed to the TV inside the cafe.

"The Palm resort," the man said. "It's all over the news."

Solomon turned back to the TV, but the report was over and now it was showing tennis highlights.

"I said, are you there?"

He brought the phone back to his ear. "Sorry, hun. I have to go."

"I'll text you when I have something. Love you!"

"I love you, too, Lilly."

He hung up, absently sliding the phone back into his pocket while all of his thoughts centered on the handgun and sniper rifle he had purchased earlier that day. Purchased from the man who sold arms to whoever was responsible for the Palm aquarium collapse.

Pieces to the puzzle were fitting together in surprising ways. If the Butler on the security footage was Simone Winifred Cassidy - and he wanted it to be - then she had to be connected somehow.

Solomon reached for his phone again and dialed the contact number he had for Murad Abdullah.

A gruff voice answered. One of the bodyguards. Solomon had been told that Murad never answered his own phone.

"Speak," the bodyguard instructed.

"My name is Solomon. I dealt with Mr. Abdullah earlier this morning."

"All deals are final."

"Wait-" he said before the man could hang up. "I just came across some information that Mr. Abdullah might find useful."

* * *

"Mr. Solomon! I am pleased to see you again so soon."

Murad Abdullah remained seated with his arms raised. He motioned for a second chair to be brought to the table.

The sun had already set and the lights of the city shone brilliantly from atop the At.Mosphere restaurant. From the 122nd floor of the Burj Khalifa, Solomon felt like a god observing his followers from the heavens.

Solomon sat, his eyes still tantalized by the perspective. "Nice view."

"I like to come here at least twice a week," Murad said. "What would you like? My cousin owns the restaurant. Order whatever you'd like."

"Thank you," Solomon said, "But I can't stay very long. I just came to deliver some information."

"And what information is this that warrants a last-minute visit?"

Solomon panned a furtive glance across the room to see who was close by. Only Murad's guards. "It's safe to talk here?"

Murad slurped down an oyster from its shell. "Of course. Like I said, my cousin owns the restaurant. You may speak freely."

Solomon didn't believe a word Murad said about his "cousins", but he spoke anyway. "You mentioned that you sold the ammunition that brought down the aquarium wall at the Palm resort?"

Murad nodded as he downed another oyster. "Experimental rounds, yes. Are you interested?"

Solomon shook his head. "No, thank you. Perhaps another time."

"Just food then?"

Solomon gave another head shake. "No, thank you. I just came from a cafe, and while I was there, I couldn't help but notice that our degrees of separation may be fewer than we had realized."

"Go on." Murad kept eating, but didn't take his eyes from Solomon.

"You see, I am here looking for someone. A woman who, according to the news report, was seen entering the Neptune Suite minutes before it was flooded."

Murad's hand paused half-way to his mouth. "Is that so?"

Solomon nodded. "The man you sold the ammo to shot at the woman I am looking for."

Puzzled, yet intrigued, Murad set his food back on the plate and wiped his hands clean. "This is quite fascinating. Quite fascinating, indeed."

"I thought you might want to know," Solomon said.

"Do you…" Murad paused, studying Solomon with narrow eyes. "What can you tell me of this woman you are searching for? Or should I say, hunting?"

"Her name is Simone Winifred Cassidy," Solomon said. "She is twenty-eight years old, five-foot-nine, has long black hair. Former star athlete at the University of Colorado Boulder back in the United States. Almost went to the Olympics for track and field competition. Born in Honolulu to parents Dominic Cassidy and Citra Locklear, both Air Force veterans, both deceased. They spent their free time hunting lost relics and preserving artifacts of antiquity. After missing the Olympic Games, Simone followed in their footsteps and soon became a noteworthy explorer and treasure hunter herself. One year ago in Monterrey, Mexico, she killed my employer, our client, and left me in the hospital with a dozen broken bones, a concussion, a ruptured spleen, and a punctured lung. And now you know why I wanted to find guns before finding her."

Murad blinked, taken aback by all of the information. "Wow," he said. "You have done your homework, I must say. Very impressive, but also very fortuitous."

"How so?"

"Your woman, Simone, she seeks the Fallen Star?" Murad slurped another oyster. "My friend, Prince Kamal, the man whose hotel suite was flooded, seeks the same prize. Why else would she break into his hotel suite?"

Solomon could see the larger picture now, not just pieces slowly fitting together. He saw the prize, the end goal for Simone.

Most importantly, he saw an opportunity.

"Can you get me in touch with your friend, the Prince?" Solomon asked.

Murad gave a short laugh, nearly choking on his bread. "Friend may have been too generous a word. Colleague, more like it. Yes, I can get you two to meet, but it scarcely seems worth the effort. He is as stubborn as a mule and twice as dumb. Thinks he can short-change me, as if I didn't see what he was up to!"

Murad huffed and ate some more, almost as if the act of consuming would drive away his hateful feelings toward Prince Kamal.

"Simone has left the country," Solomon said. "I'm working on tracking her location, but if I could meet with the Prince and learn what he knows, I can bring you the Fallen Star."

A grin drove away Murad's scowl. "You can do that?"

Solomon nodded slowly, with confidence.

"Prince Kamal has a scroll, provided it didn't get lost in the flood," Murad said. "He tried to sell it to me in place of the Star itself. Of course, I demanded he leave and return with the real thing."

"Put me in touch with him and I will find it," Solomon said. "If I can get to the location before Simone and her crew, I'll take them out and bring you the Fallen Star."

Murad wiped his hands vigorously and tossed the napkin aside. "Very well! What sort of price are you looking at?"

"None," Solomon said.

Murad's expression went from excitement to shock. "You want *nothing*? Surely, there is some way I can repay you for your troubles - should you succeed, of course."

Solomon gave it a moment's consideration. There was nothing he wanted. Except…

"Two guns might not be enough," he said. "What else can you spare?"

A devilish grin twisted into to Murad's face. He stood for the first time, offering his hand to Solomon.

They shook.

18.

Thessaly, Greece

They rode the horses in silence as the black sky gradually shifted to a shade of deep indigo.

Despite having not been on a horse in twenty years, Simone rode along with little trouble. The animal was tame and seemingly content in its duty of transporting Simone to the Meteora monasteries.

She shuddered to think what she would have done if the only mode of transport was an automobile.

A part of her believed she wouldn't have gone, but another part knew she would have broken the decades-long boycott of riding in a wheeled motor vehicle. After all, she considered just then, that was how she was transported to the hospital.

Damn.

She hadn't even thought about that. There had been too many other pressing concerns vying for attention. She vaguely recalled protesting, but the memory was nebulous and unclear. Despite her fear of getting into a car or van or truck or ambulance, she had arrived at the hospital safe and sound.

Shaking the thoughts from her head, Simone concentrated on something else. Something to take her mind off the ambulance ride. Coming to the front of her thoughts was the question she had long been avoiding…

What am I doing here?

She never wanted to come along. She had only wanted to speak with Clark, who made himself conveniently absent when she did arrive at Andrews AFB. Any thoughts she'd harbored of bargaining had been left on the tarmac when the plane took off to ship her to the Czech Republic.

She had thought things would be different this time, and they certainly were, in all the wrong ways.

An overwhelming feeling of regret passed through Simone, nearly bringing tears to her eyes. It left her feeling out of her element, lost in a life that wasn't hers to live. Trapped in a sequence of events that she wasn't supposed to be a part of.

She reminded herself that she was a treasure hunter, and there was an antiquity of vital importance just ahead, that everything she had accomplished thus far and everything she had gone through would be worth it once she set her hands on the Fallen Star.

But no matter how much she reminded herself of this, negative feelings crept in. In place of the wild, she had attempted to rob a grave under a church, caused the ruin of a luxury vacation resort, and was now en route to a peaceful and secluded monastery to do who knows what.

She wondered if it was merely the lack of sleep affecting her, or if the thoughts and feelings coursing through her in that moment had true validity.

One thing she knew for certain. One thing had not changed.

This was her last mission with Clark's crew.

She didn't need Clark; Clark needed her. Whatever she had to do to avoid him or Lincoln or April or anyone else from their unit finding her, she would do it. She'd hole up in some uncharted corner of the globe and scour the pages of her parents' travel journal until she knew with concrete certainty where to go next.

She needed to get away, recharge, and get back on the right track.

"Simone."

She turned her head in puzzlement.

Lincoln's eyes stared into her. "I asked if you were all right."

"Oh, sorry," she said. "I was daydreaming."

April rode up beside Simone. "You look terrible."

"Really?"

She didn't feel terrible. Only tired, but not sleepy. Tired in the sense that every time she moved her body, it felt sore. Fatigued was the right word, she decided.

"I'm fine," she said to convince the others as much as herself.

"Are you sure?" Lincoln asked.

"Fine enough to play the role of the ill nun."

She thought of the robes they had been given by the family at the stable, curious to know how good a disguise they would be, wondering if riding into the monastery wearing their adventure gear would be enough to sell the lie, if robes would be an over-sell.

Another stretch of silence grew as they rode. Time passed in amorphous fashion. Simone couldn't tell a minute from an hour. She kept looking up at the sky to gauge their passage by the changing colors in the clouds.

Dawn yet lingered beyond the horizon.

She felt herself nodding off, then startling awake as she remembered she was on a horse and had to be careful not to fall off. An acute craving for sleep mingled with the desire to remain awake, knowing full well what visions awaited her slumber.

Nearly a year later, the sight of Heather Severn bleeding out in the Aztec cave still shook her to her core. Every time she slept, she still heard the sound of the gunshot she had fired that took the life of another man, a person she didn't know anything about. She heard that shot as loudly as she had on the day her finger squeezed the trigger. She would awake with ears ringing, sweat pouring down her face and saturating her hair.

She hadn't had a real sleep since she drowned in Dubai. She did everything she could not to think about whether or not she would feel those same sensations again the next time she closed her eyes. Those terrifying sensations of her lungs unable to hold a breath, of water rushing down her throat, choking as it filled her lungs.

Simone shivered at the thought.

"We should be almost there," Lincoln said, as if he knew what was going through her mind just then.

Looking ahead, Simone was struck with a wave of nausea. Her head felt stuck in the clouds. Her pulse quickened and she found herself sweating, yet cold at the same time.

She breathed deeper, focusing on staying on the horse as it moved over the uneven dirt path.

Searching her memories, she couldn't recall taking any sleeping pills or painkillers since they had left the plane over an hour ago. She thought maybe she just needed food, but her stomach felt as if it was preparing to regurgitate what little was in there.

Swaying unsteadily on the horse, Simone found herself in free-fall with the ground coming up quick.

"*Simone!*"

Shouts of her name echoed far away as her eyes drifted shut.

* * *

Simone opened her eyes to faint daylight bleeding into a cloudless sky.

Lincoln and April's heads hovered in front of her vision, which instantly reminded Simone of the stereotypical scene from a movie when someone wakes after being rendered unconscious.

"Simone, are you okay?" Lincoln asked.

She blinked, looked about, and nodded. "Yeah, I'm fine."

April did not look convinced. "That's what you were saying right before you fell off your horse."

Simone glanced at the ground under her, not realizing she had, indeed, fallen from her mount.

She pressed her palms into the grassy dirt and attempted to stand. "I'm just fine," she said.

Getting to her feet, Simone stumbled, her legs like jelly. Lincoln and April caught her, holding her up and steadying her.

"What happened?" Lincoln asked.

"I just got lightheaded," she replied. "I'll be okay. I just need to eat something, I think."

Simone moved to a large rock that she was thankful she missed in her plunge from the horse, and sat down. April gave her a protein bar.

"Eat this."

Simone took the bar. "Thanks."

She ate under the skeptical glare of Lincoln. Looking away, Simone considered that she had simply pushed herself too hard, too quickly. Her habit of self-medication certainly didn't help her condition, nor did it help her sleep on the plane, which was the reason for doing so in the first place.

She scarfed down the protein bar, already feeling better than before she fell. She stood. Lincoln reached out but she batted his hand away.

Simone got to her horse and climbed on unassisted.

"Are we going?" she asked.

Lincoln traded a look with April. They mounted their horses and continued onward.

It wasn't long before a vast and sweeping valley spread out before them. Simone could already see the monasteries perched atop perilous rock formations in the distance.

"Looks like we made it," April said.

Lincoln slowed his horse, gazing at the impressive view. Two of the six monasteries were situated nearby, with the other four standing farther north in the valley.

"Which one do you think it is?" he asked no one in particular.

"That one." Simone pointed to the less accessible of the two nearby. "The larger ones are farther north. If I was going to hide something, it wouldn't be where the most people would be."

Lincoln looked to April to see what her opinion was.

"I agree," April said. "I wouldn't make it that easy."

Lincoln looked ahead, his eyes shifting between the two nearest monasteries. One seemed undoubtedly more accessible, resting on a plateau a short distance from the valley below. The other had been built atop a sheer spire of rock jutting vertically into the sky. It almost seemed impossible that it had been built where it was.

"Okay," Lincoln said to the others, and they continued in the direction of the monastery perched atop the rocky cliff.

Simone was feeling much more herself by the time they arrived at the base of the cliff. She was relieved to see that steps had been carved directly into the rock itself, winding a pathway up to the top. It meant they didn't have to leave the horses below. They could ride upward and see that they were cared for while undergoing the covert operation to locate and retrieve the Fallen Star.

Provided, of course, that Simone had chosen the correct monastery.

April handed out the robes they had acquired. They threw them on over their clothes without dismounting.

Simone looked at the others. "This could actually work."

"We'll find out when we get up there," April said as she held out her arms to see that, luckily, none of her tattoos were visible.

Lincoln readied himself before the steps. "Sister Farren, Sister Cassidy, are you ready?"

"Just ride, Father Lewis," April said with a hint of irritation on her voice.

The horses had less difficulty than Simone had assumed they would scaling the steps. It was no easy task to reach the top, but more than a hundred and thirty steps later, Simone, Lincoln, and April found themselves in a wide and open courtyard before the main building.

A man in his sixties, with a dark robe and a round, black hat, watched from a window on the second story. His only hair was on his chin.

Lincoln and April dismounted. The duo then helped Simone from her horse to play up the charade.

Simone raised her eyes to take in the surroundings.

The building before them stood two stories and stretched from one side of the cliff to the other. Several smaller buildings were connected on either side. Behind, the complex appeared to extend to the opposite end of the cliff, building on top of itself as it went. To Simone's eyes, every individual building seemed connected to another to create one massive monastery.

She was about to say how they had their work cut out for them when two other monks, dressed in dark robes, round hats, and beards, emerged from one of the smaller structures adjacent to the main building.

"Greetings, travelers," said one of them with his arms spread in welcome. "My name is Argus, and this is Paulos."

"Father Lewis, Sister Farren," Lincoln said, indicating himself and April. He looked to Simone. "Sister Cassidy is in ill health."

"Come inside, friends," Argus said. "We have food and medicine. Come."

Argus and Paulos led the way past a series of arches and through the doors of The Monastery of the Holy Trinity.

As Simone walked with the aid of Lincoln and April, she saw from the corner of her vision the watchful eye of the monk in the second-story window. He made no move to help. He simply watched, expressionless, giving no indication that Simone and the others were welcome there.

19.

Thessaly, Greece

"How many of you are here?" Lincoln asked as he took a sip of water from the cup Argus had given him.

"Six," Argus said. He gave April a cup of water and smiled.

"Only six? For this entire place?" Lincoln said. "That's a lot to manage."

Argus sat at the table opposite Lincoln and April. "We have nothing but time up here."

Lincoln listened to Argus ramble on about how they grew their own crops, mended their own clothes, brewed their own beer, and maintained all the properties of the monastery. All the while, his thoughts went to Simone, whom he had watched disappear down a hallway with the help of Paulos.

He'd protested and urged that he needed to be by Simone's side, but Argus was steadfast in allowing his monks to tend to Sister Cassidy's wound and provide the medicine she needed.

Neither Lincoln nor April explained what had happened to Simone. They kept the story vague on purpose, only answering questions about her when asked directly.

Just as Lincoln thought about how to allow access for himself and April into the deeper recesses of the complex, Argus said, "How long will you be staying with us, Father Lewis?"

"Just until Sister Cassidy is well enough to travel." He almost said Simone, but caught himself just in time.

"Very well." Argus stood. "Shall I show you to your quarters?"

Lincoln rose to his feet. "I'd very much like to see how Sister Cassidy is doing, if possible."

Argus motioned to the interior door. "It is on the way. I will take you."

* * *

Simone winced as Paulos inspected her lacerated calf.

"Does that hurt?" he asked in a voice both deep and soft.

"A little."

She reclined on a mattress made of straw. The room she had been taken to was starkly barren. No decorations hung on the walls, and there was no furniture apart from the uncomfortable bed and one dresser. Her bag had been carried in by another monk and left on the stone floor by the door.

"How did this happen?" Paulos asked.

"Glass," Simone said, keeping her story simple. She nearly laughed as she wondered how he would react if she did, in fact, tell the truth.

Paulos had by his side a medical tote which reminded Simone of what doctors of old carried with them on house calls. It was just large enough to hold the bare essentials.

Paulos raised a flashlight to Simone's left eye, then shifted the light to her right eye. He listened to her heart, felt the pulse at her wrist, looked into her ears and down her throat. The monk seemed to know exactly what he was doing.

"Are you the doctor here?" Simone asked.

"Please, relax."

A few minutes later, Paulos packed up his medical bag and set it aside.

"You must rest," he said. "I will bring you something to help you sleep."

Simone sat up. "That's quite all right. I slept on the way here."

"You must sleep more. Your body is weak." He picked up his medical bag and stood. "I will bring you something for sleep."

Before Simone could get in another word, Paulos was out the door and gone, leaving her alone in the room that reminded her of a medieval prison.

She threw her legs over the side of the bed and got to her feet, gazing about. The one feature that set her room apart from a medieval prison was the single window at the opposite end of the small room.

Simone walked to the window, her legs feeling steadier than before, and peered out.

The room, she found, was situated at the end of the cliff. The window looked just wide enough for her to squeeze out if she had to, but as she leaned over, she saw that there was nowhere for her to go if she did climb out. A sheer drop awaited, plunging straight down to the valley hundreds and hundreds of feet below.

Now she began feeling as if this had, indeed, been a prison at some point in the past.

Simone went to the door and tested the handle. It wasn't locked.

She decided this wasn't the right time to go meandering about. She had to prove she was healthy enough first. She didn't know what form of medical training Paulos had, but he saw enough to know that she was weak and short of sleep, even from his rudimentary examination.

Not even so much as a mirror hung on the walls. The monks had no use for vanity, she considered as she felt her face, wondering exactly how terrible she looked.

There has to be a bathroom somewhere around here, she thought.

Simone went to the door again, but stopped dead in her tracks as it opened without her touching it.

As the door opened, she saw a figure standing in the hall, cloaked in the black robes and wearing the black hat of the monks. A silver sash was tied around his waist. His head was bald but his beard was long, peppered with equal parts black and grey.

Simone's breath caught in the back of her throat as she realized this was the man who had been watching from the window.

"You're up," he said with slight surprise.

"I thought I heard someone coming."

He stepped into the room. "I'm sorry if I startled you, my child. Forgive me. My name is Demetrius."

"I'm-"

"Sister Cassidy," he said before she could get the words out. "And you should be in bed. Please, rest." He waved an arm toward the bed.

Simone sat on the edge of the straw mattress. "Thank you for your hospitality. I'm feeling much better already."

"Brother Paulos believes otherwise." Demetrius moved to the bed and sat beside Simone. "And when it comes to matters of health, I put my complete and unwavering trust in Brother Paulos."

"He's very kind," Simone said, not knowing what else to say.

Demetrius studied Simone's hair, which hung freely over her shoulders.

"I usually wear my hair up," she lied. "It came undone when I fell."

"Fell?"

"Fell ill," she said, trying to get her story straight. "I was in and out of sleep for a while. I hardly remember getting here."

"Which is why you must rest," Demetrius said. "I will make sure you have everything you need brought to you. You won't even have to leave the bed."

"Is there a … place to wash up?"

Demetrius smiled. "It is just across the hall."

"Thank you. You're very kind to take us in," Simone said. "I promise we won't burden you for long."

"You are no burden to us," he said. "We live to serve."

Demetrius rose from the bed at the sound of the door opening. Paulos carried in a steaming cup and brought it to Simone.

Demetrius crossed the room to exit. "Rest, my child."

He left Simone alone with Paulos, who offered her the cup.

"Drink," he urged.

Simone took the cup in her hands. It was hot to the touch, but it felt good on her fingers and palms.

"What is it?" she asked.

"It will help you sleep."

Simone raised the cup to her mouth. It smelled sweet, almost floral. She raised her eyes to Paulos and gave a short laugh. "It's very warm."

"It is best when it is warm."

He made no move to leave, instead hovering close to the bed to witness Simone take the first sip.

Knowing he wasn't going to leave until she drank, Simone brought the cup to her lips and took a small sip.

She felt the hot liquid burning its way through her as she swallowed.

"Wow," she said. "Very warm."

"It will warm you up, yes," Paulos said. "Please, drink."

Again, the monk waited for her.

Simone drank a more generous sip. She felt a tingling in her arms and legs. Part of her thought it was her imagination, triggered by the thought that she had no idea what she was drinking and that she didn't trust Demetrius any more than she trusted Clark Bannicheck.

She drank some more, the cup now halfway empty.

Paulos smiled. Satisfied, he left the room, urging her one last time to sleep and get well-rested before he disappeared down the hallway.

Simone set the hot cup on the floor and leaned back on the bed.

Whatever she was drinking, it made her realize just how starved for sleep she truly was. She pushed herself up to a seated position, but decided against standing. Her head was getting light again and she felt, strangely, as if she was high.

Did this monk drug me?

She thought she was about to panic, but her muscles relaxed and her heartbeat remained steady. Then it felt as if she was floating downward, into the bed, sinking into the pillow, and suddenly the mattress wasn't so uncomfortable anymore.

As her eyes slipped shut, all she could think about was finding the Fallen Star.

20.

Thessaly, Greece

Simone awoke with a start, lurching up and falling from the bed.

Grunting as she hit the cold stone floor, she pushed herself up on her hands and knees. She awoke suddenly as always, but this time it was different. She wasn't startled by a nightmarish vision from the past. Instead, she scared herself into wondering why such a vision had not come.

Simone got to her feet with assistance from the bed, and stretched her arms out to her sides as she yawned. Her first decent sleep in forever.

What the hell was in that cup?

Simone picked the cup off the floor and smelled what remained inside. She thought about drinking the rest and hoping to get just a bit more sleep, but no, she had to find the Fallen Star. She'd already wasted too much time sleeping.

Now wasn't the time to rest, she realized, and spilled the rest of the concoction out the window. Now was the time to act.

Feeling rejuvenated, Simone dug into her bag for fresh clothes. She found them along with an airplane bottle of whiskey.

Holding the bottle in her hand, she thought about taking it with her. The longer she thought about it, she more she felt precious time dripping away - time that could be spent searching the complex.

Simone made up her mind, and took the whiskey bottle with her to the washroom across the hall.

She emerged minutes later wearing clean cargo pants and a dark tee-shirt. She slipped across the hall and ducked into the room where she had slept.

The robe she'd been given at the stable smelled of horses. She tossed it onto the bed and elected to prowl the monastery without her disguise. There couldn't be too many monks around. She'd read that their numbers had dwindled over the years. The few who remained shouldn't be too difficult to evade.

Simone strapped her knife to her belt - just in case.

She eased the door open, checking the hall for anyone passing by, listening for footsteps echoing off the cold stone.

The coast was clear.

She made one last check in her pockets to make sure she had everything she might need. Flashlight, lighter, knife on her belt, whiskey, cell phone - even though there was no reception on top of the precipitous rock formation - and a walkie-talkie for communicating with April and Lincoln.

With a deep breath, Simone crept from her room and down the hall, peeking into every room she passed after listening for movement within. She felt more and more like her imaginary secret agent alter ego, Rosa Munroe. As silly as it was, the thought gave her confidence to keep moving.

She hadn't considered where Lincoln and April might be. Perhaps eating something, which was what she should be doing, she realized. But food would have to wait. She didn't know when she'd have another opportunity to sneak off on her own undetected.

This might be her only chance.

Simone checked inside numerous bedrooms and storage areas but found nothing that would give a hint that an antiquity of historic significance was there at all.

She ducked into a dark stairwell at the sound of footfalls approaching.

Crouching low on the stairs, Simone peered through the crack between the door and the floor as a monk walked by and kept walking.

Simone waited, listening. The footsteps faded.

She rose to her feet, but a strange noise came to her just then, something far off, as if it was inside her head. She thought it must be an echo in the stairwell, or a sound from one of the rooms below, likely dedicated to providing whatever rudimentary water or power they had at the old facility.

But as the sound grew from a distant hum to a rumble nearby, Simone was struck by the urge to find a window as quickly as possible to see if her fear had come true.

She raced back into the hall and into the nearest room she was certain was empty. It faced the courtyard where she had arrived with the others.

Craning her neck up to see into the sky, Simone couldn't spot it but knew what it was and where it was going.

A helicopter.

And it was coming in to land.

The rumble was now a roar as the monstrous steel beast hovered lower and lower, finally coming to rest in the courtyard. The sigil emblazoned on the side brought forth memories of the dagger April had taken from the Brno Ossuary.

The symbol of Prince Orimer Kamal.

"Oh, crap."

Simone spun away from the window, hands balled into fists. "Dammit, now what?"

Think, Simone, think!

* * *

Lincoln jumped up and ran to the nearest window at the sound of the helicopter approaching.

April turned from where she sat at the table. "What is it?" she asked, knowing the answer to her own question but remaining true to her role in the presence of Argus.

Lincoln watched as the chopper drew nearer. "Helicopter."

He locked eyes with April. A moment of silent understanding passed between them. They had to do something.

"Helicopter?" Argus went to the window and peered out.

"Are you expecting anyone?" Lincoln asked.

While the monk's attention was distracted, Lincoln mouthed the words *the prince* to April.

April mouthed an obscenity.

Paulos rushed into the room, a worried expression turned toward Lincoln.

"She's gone from her room," he said.

"Sister Cassidy?" Lincoln exchanged glances with April once more.

He wasn't sure how long to keep up the charade, and judging by April's look, she wasn't sure, either. Knowing her, she would be ready to blow it up at that very moment if that's what had to be done.

Lincoln stepped over to Paulos. "We must find her. She is not feeling well."

Argus turned away from the window as the noise of the helicopter grew to a deafening volume. "Do you know these people?" he shouted.

Lincoln shook his head.

In fact, they didn't know him, either. It hit him - nobody in the Prince's cadre knew him at all. But they'd seen April.

"Sister Farren, perhaps it's best you check on Sister Cassidy."

April got the hint. She wasted no time following Paulos out of the room en route to Simone's bunk.

Argus watched as the chopper landed, spinning down its rotor blades. "I wonder who it could be…"

"I'll stay here," Lincoln said. He went back to the table where the group had been sitting before the disturbance arose.

Without a word, Argus started off to greet the incoming travelers.

God dammit.

He'd thought Simone was still fast asleep as she had been when he was taken by her room a short while ago. She'd appeared to be in full hibernation, getting the best sleep of her life. And she needed it.

Lincoln fought the urge to stand up and watch from the window, but doing so would only draw suspicion. He had to appear normal.

Unless the Prince came in with all guns blazing.

Lincoln felt naked without a weapon by his side. It would be easy enough to conceal one beneath his robes, if only his gear wasn't stashed away in the room he'd been given.

Instead, he sat and listened, hoping April would be able to sneak something past Paulos and bring it back quickly.

He listened but couldn't hear a damn thing over the chopper blades whirring down. He knew words were exchanged, but it was impossible to make out a single one.

Before he knew it, Argus stepped through the door, ushering in his newest guests.

"Father Lewis, this is Prince Kamal and his colleagues."

Lincoln stood to greet them, forcing a smile and playing the role he needed to play. "Greetings, Prince Kamal."

He shook the hands of everyone walking into the room - the Prince, and all four of his "colleagues".

Judging by the semi-automatic weapons concealed under their garments, Lincoln knew exactly what their purpose was.

Protect the Prince at all costs, and prevent anyone else from retrieving the Fallen Star.

"Please, sit." Argus motioned the Prince to the common table.

Prince Kamal sat at the head of the table, barely acknowledging Lincoln's presence. A mere peon. Nobody worth worrying about.

"A busy day," Argus said with a smile. "A busy day, indeed. This is most unusual."

"Unusual in what way?" Prince Kamal asked.

Argus sat. He raised a hand toward Lincoln. "Our friend, Father Lewis, is also seeking refuge."

"We were traveling on a pilgrimage from Athens when one of the Sisters took ill," Lincoln said. "Brother Argus was kind enough to allow us to rest awhile."

Prince Kamal didn't seem to hear or care.

"You are also having difficulty in your trip?" Lincoln asked in an attempt to pry more information out of the Prince.

"Our helicopter is low on fuel," he said. "I have sent two men to the nearest city."

"It's fortunate you were able to find a place to land on short notice," Lincoln said.

"Fortune appears to smile in my direction this day," the Prince declared.

Argus poured a glass of water for each of the new arrivals. "I can fix you up with a room if you'd like to rest."

"That will not be necessary. We intend to get what we need and leave at once."

"A busy man," Argus said. "One should always find the time for leisure. Fortune has gifted you this opportunity, Prince Kamal."

He didn't acknowledge the remark. He simply drank his water and then stood.

"My colleagues would like to be shown around. They have never been to a place such as this. Could you grant them a tour of the grounds?"

Argus smiled and rose to his feet. "I will, gladly." He looked to Lincoln. "We shouldn't be long. Make yourself at home."

Three of the bodyguards followed Argus out of the room. The one remaining sat across from Lincoln.

Prince Kamal resumed his seat at the head of the table.

* * *

Lighting on the lower level was dim. The monks seemed to rely on electricity only for necessity, and never for convenience.

Simone had chosen to retreat down the stairs, deeper under the monastery. Not only would she be harder to find, but she figured that anyone looking to keep something secret wouldn't have it sitting out in the open.

She didn't expect the system of tunnels running underneath the monastery to be so vast and complex. The excavated area below the structure must be as large as the buildings themselves.

Most of the areas she came to were for the storage of grain and equipment for brewing beer. The small LED flashlight she held in her hand was often the only source of light.

Simone pressed onward, deeper into the maze of narrow corridors and low ceilings. Every time she panned the light to see what lay ahead, she expected to see something hiding in the dark, something ready to leap out and attack.

But she was alone.

Simone paused, listening for sounds above. The stone was thick and kept any noise from penetrating.

She couldn't hear anything except her own breathing. Not even the helicopter. All was deadly quiet below the monastery.

Looking to the walkie-talkie at her hip, she turned it on. There were two others - one for Lincoln and the other for April. Simone felt it best to be ready for when one of them decided to check in.

If they ever got the opportunity.

Simone came to the end of a hallway that bent at a right angle, continued for six feet, then abruptly stopped. She stared at the sheer face of a rock wall.

"Weird."

Why would the monks carve a hallway into nowhere? Maybe it was for future expansion?

Something in the back of Simone's head told her this wasn't right.

She pressed against the wall but it wouldn't budge no matter how hard she pushed. Instead, she knocked against it with the palm of her hand. It sounded solid.

Simone stepped back, not giving up just yet. There was no other instance of a hallway or corridor in the entire complex that she saw coming to a stop for no reason. Exhaling through her nose, Simone traced the wall with her flashlight, running the beam along the corners from one end all the way up and around to the other.

She stopped, holding the light steadily.

Leaning in for a closer inspection, she saw it clearly.

A crack in the rock. Nearly imperceptible, it ran all along the corner of the wall, as if the wall had been fitted into place exactly. She brought her finger to the seam, feeling it to make sure she wasn't just seeing things.

No, this was real. An actual seam in the rock. That meant there had once been a passageway beyond the wall. The hallway didn't just end. It had been blocked off.

With a ripple of excitement coursing through her, Simone bit down on the flashlight and used both hands to feel along the seam, searching for some kind of mechanism that might trigger the movement of the stone wall.

Nothing. It was flush all around.

"Hmm…"

Thinking, Simone took the light from her mouth and aimed it at the walls beside her.

Two square stones had been set into the wall, flush and hardly noticeable in the darkness. She looked over the wall again just to make sure she wasn't missing anything.

The two square stones were situated side-by-side with several inches separating them.

"Well, here goes nothing…"

Simone held her breath and pushed into the square nearest the wall. It depressed into the wall three inches but would go no further.

Simone watched as nothing happened.

She let go of the stone and pressed the second square.

This time, a rumble sounded from within the passageway that had been blocked off. With a colossal groan, the massive rock wall began sliding sideways, gradually, painfully slow, inches at a time, stone grinding against stone.

Simone let go and waited for the wall to move fully aside.

But once her hand was removed from the square, the wall began sliding back into place.

The wall set itself back in place with a solid *thud*, sealing the hallway once again.

"Awesome," Simone said. "That's really awesome."

There was no way everyone above didn't hear that wall sliding and thudding and grinding and making the most noise possible.

There also seemed to be no way to get the wall to stay open. Someone had to stand outside and hold the square rock.

Simone hadn't been able to catch a glimpse of anything beyond the wall. It was as dark as sleep. Without knowing if there was any control on the other side to operate the door, she might end up stuck beyond an immovable slab of stone.

Thinking on her feet, Simone backtracked, searching each storage area for something large and strong enough to brace the door and keep it from closing all the way.

She paused every thirty seconds, waiting for the inevitable sound of footsteps descending to investigate the sound.

Nobody came.

After five minutes of searching, Simone found a boulder the size of her torso in a room with a damaged wall. She thought it might work just by looking at it, giving thanks for the disrepair of the tunnels beneath the seven-hundred year old site. When she tried to move it, she knew it would work for sure.

At far less than optimal strength, Simone had to strain herself and dig deep to find the power within to even make the boulder budge from the spot where it had rested, likely for dozens and dozens of years.

Rolling the boulder down the hall to the stone door, Simone gasped for breath and took a seat on the boulder itself once she had positioned it near where the door opened.

Sweat dripped from her brow. She could feel her shirt sticking to her from the exertion. But it was cool below ground and she was thankful for that.

Listening again, Simone heard nobody approaching.

She wasn't sure if that was good or bad.

They have to have heard it...

Whatever was going on topside, it was preoccupying everyone enough that Simone was allowed to operate without interruption. She'd almost hoped that someone would come looking for her. At least then she'd know that things up top were somewhat normal.

Once her heart rate slowed, Simone stood and rolled the boulder closer to the wall.

Simone held her breath again as she pressed into the square that had opened the door the first time.

Once again, the door groaned and began grinding sideways, revealing a cold, dark passage beyond.

Simone cringed at the loudness of the wall sliding away, but she had to get it open far enough to have time to move the boulder into place.

Once the wall was more than half-way open, Simone let go of the square, rushed to the boulder, and shoved with all her might.

The big round boulder rolled into the opening as the stone wall was grinding its way closed. Simone didn't like how it closed faster than it had opened.

She watched with bated breath as the huge stone wall impacted the boulder.

Wedged between the wall and the closing door, the boulder held firm. The wall stopped sliding shut.

Simone tested the stability of the boulder with her foot, making sure it would hold.

Satisfied, Simone took a deep breath and pressed her back as tightly against the wall as possible.

"Please don't crush me," she said as she eased one foot over the boulder and into the darkness beyond.

Emptying her lungs and making herself as thin as possible, Simone squeezed her torso between the wall and the stone door.

Ever so slowly, Simone eased herself through, feeling the cold rock against her in front and behind. She had centimeters of leeway. One wrong nudge and the door could shove the boulder aside and turn her into human jelly.

Simone was almost through. She could feel her heart beating against the stone door as her chest scraped past.

Finally, her torso past the threshold, Simone brought her other foot carefully through.

Standing beyond the blocked passageway, Simone took a much-needed deep breath, raised the flashlight, and gazed into the unknown.

One second later, the flashlight flickered.

"Come on…"

She clicked it off and back on again. It sputtered to life.

Again she raised the light, and again the light went out.

"Son of a… come on come on come on, not now…"

Simone clicked it off and on again, but nothing happened. She tried shaking it, batting the end against her palm, but nothing worked.

Shivering from a sudden chill, clutching a broken flashlight, Simone stood in absolute darkness.

21.

Thessaly, Greece

Lincoln waited for Argus to return but he did not come.

"I should check on the others," he said. "They've been gone a while. I hope Sister Cassidy is all right."

Prince Kamal stood suddenly, rising to his feet before Lincoln had the chance to do the same. "I, too, have grown tired of waiting."

Lincoln eased himself up, careful not to startle the remaining bodyguard. "The tour is very brief. There isn't much to see. Your friends should be back any minute now."

"I do not have time to spend idly," the Prince said. He threw his gaze to the bodyguards. "Let us find it and be gone."

He was through the door and into the inner complex of rooms before Lincoln could get another word out.

He followed not far behind the Prince, hanging back a safe distance should anything violent begin up ahead.

Lincoln had several handguns stashed away in his bag and in April's, but they were on the other side of the monastery. He only knew one way through. There had to be another on the outside, but he didn't want to chance looking suspicious in front of the Prince's private helicopter pilot, who lingered in the vehicle, waiting for the others to return.

Lincoln had to get to the bag in his room. Not only for the guns, but for the walkie-talkie.

He followed behind as the Prince threw doors open and stormed away dissatisfied with each room he happened upon. How long a man of his type would maintain patience before the semi-automatic weapons began firing, Lincoln didn't know, but he expected it wasn't much longer.

Prince Kamal turned right and continued that way, toward a part of the complex that Lincoln hadn't yet seen.

He took the chance, slipping by and hurrying now toward his room.

Strangely, he saw no one on his way. Not any of the six monks, none of the three other bodyguards, not April, and not Simone. It was as if the place had suddenly been evacuated, leaving him there alone.

Struck with the feeling that something bad was imminent, Lincoln got to his quarters in a hurry and closed the door. He tore open his bag on the bed and found the two handguns inside along with the walkie-talkie.

He checked both guns. Both were fully loaded. He slipped one into the back of his pants under his robe and kept the other close by on the firm straw mattress.

Clicking on the walkie-talkie, he checked the channel to make sure it was dialed in correctly. It was. He hit the button to speak.

"Check check check, anyone hearing me? Over."

He waited an eternity, his eyes watching the door. He wiped his sweaty palms on his robe.

Nobody came to the door, and nobody answ-

"Hello? Lincoln, is that you?"

It was Simone's voice.

"Yes, yes, it's me. Where the hell are you? Over."

He felt his heart rate rising. The adrenaline was making him too warm. He tore off the robe that reeked of horse stink and threw it aside.

"Underneath you," Simone said through a crackle of static.

Underneath? Lincoln wasn't sure he understood. "Underneath the monastery? Over."

"Yeah, I found some stairs. I'm not sure where. I backed into them in a hurry trying to lay low. Yeah, over."

Lincoln held his eyes fixed on the door, waiting for the slightest movement. "Are you in a safe place? If you're not, get to one right now. Over."

There was a pause on the other line. Then, "Yeah, about that…"

Lincoln hesitated before replying. "About what? What's wrong?"

He ditched the formality of communications jargon that had been drilled into him during his military days.

"I'm probably in the safest possible place right now," Simone said. "It's so safe, I can't even find myself."

"What do you mean?"

"I mean it's pitch black my effin' flashlight went out. I can't even see my hand in front of my own face."

Lincoln sighed. He had put the new batteries into all the flashlights personally. Brand new. There was no reason it shouldn't be working, but it wasn't, and it was his fault.

"I'm sorry," he said. "Stay where you are. I'll find you."

"You can't be far," she said. "Just look for a staircase. It's the only one I saw."

"I'll be as quick as I can. Out."

Lincoln clicked his walkie-talkie off so it didn't give away his position as he moved.

He got up, taking the gun from his bed and switching the safety off. He crept up to the door and listened with his ear to the weathered old wood.

No sound from the other side.

Carefully, he placed his hand on the latch and eased the door open, stifling the creak of the rusted hinges as best as he could.

He poked his head into the hallway. The coast was clear. He stepped out, gun in hand, finger hovering away from the trigger, ready to fire if he had to.

Drawing a long, steady breath, he patted his pocket to make sure he had his flashlight on him to trade with Simone. Thankfully, he did.

Lincoln slunk closer to April's room, curious to know if she was hiding there or not.

He stopped at her door, listening for sounds from within.

No sound.

He pressed down on the door latch and carefully pushed the door open. If she hadn't yet grabbed her walkie-talkie and a gun, he'd grab them in case their paths met.

Inching the door open, Lincoln slipped inside.

He stopped cold as the hard metal of a gun barrel was pressed firmly against his head.

"Son of a bitch, god dammit, Lincoln," April said, pulling the gun away from his face.

Lincoln gently closed the door. "Thanks for not shooting me."

Inside the room with April was Paulos, looking confused and helpless.

"Where are the others?" April asked. "The Prince and his goons?"

"They took off," Lincoln said in a low voice as he lingered by the door, waiting for any disturbance on the other side.

"Took off where?" she asked.

"Don't know. Probably to find what they came looking for."

"What would that be? The fuel?" Paulos didn't understand.

April turned to the monk. "They're looking for something you probably don't even know you have."

"And we're here to make sure they don't get it," Lincoln added.

Paulos shook his head. "Forgive me, but you must explain to me. What do we have here that is so important to this man? We are here to maintain a peaceful life, a life free from extravagances and luxury. We are simple men working with simple tools. If this man is a prince, surely he can buy whatever he came here in search of, no?"

"No," April said frankly.

Lincoln stepped toward them. "Hold on."

"Hold on to what?" April argued.

"What if it's really not here?" he asked. "Think about it."

The thought hit April like a truck. She looked ready to explode. They came all this way for nothing?

Lincoln locked eyes with Paulos. "The Prince is looking for an ancient artifact. He was in possession of a scroll found in the Brno Ossuary in the Czech Republic."

Solemnly, Paulos shook his head. "We have no such artifacts here."

April fixed the monk with a burning stare. "The scroll said it was here. The Prince tracked it here independently from us. We all came to the same conclusion, and you're telling me you don't have it?"

Paulos raised his arms in a shrug. "I don't even know what *it* is you are referring to. A scroll found in an ossuary? I don't have any knowledge of this."

Lincoln chewed his lip as he traded a look with April, a look of disappointment mixed with simmering agitation.

"Would Argus know?" he asked the monk. "Would anyone else here know about it?"

"No, not at all. As I have said, we harbor no ancient antiquities here. That is not our purpose."

April stormed across the room. "This was nothing but a waste. A huge waste of time."

She tore off her robe and flung it away. Letting her hair down, she passed Lincoln and waited by the door, gun at the ready.

"Let's go," she said. "Let the idiot prince look for it if it's not here. Where's Simone?"

"Underneath us."

April raised a confused stare to Lincoln. "In the valley?"

"No, I mean downstairs."

April just stared, confused.

"She found a staircase," Lincoln said. "I had her on the walkie a minute ago. She's in the dark without a light."

"Great," she said.

Gun in hand, Lincoln waved to the door. "Make sure the Prince's bodyguards aren't lurking out there."

He turned to the monk.

"Do you know how to get to the-"

Before he could get the word 'staircase' out, Paulos took Lincoln's gun right out of his hand. It was effortless, as Lincoln never expected the monk to make a move for it.

"Don't move." Paulos raised the gun to April.

She turned, only then realizing what had happened.

Lincoln looked at him in disbelief. "Paulos..."

"Put the gun on the floor and kick it to me."

April stood her ground. "You've gotta be f-"

"Do it now or I will shoot," he demanded, his voice firm and confident.

Lincoln swallowed the lump in his throat as he watched the monk handle the firearm with expertise. The way he held his arm out, the way his hand gripped the weapon, the way his breath remained steady.

This man had been trained.

April scoffed, but complied. She leaned over, holding the gun by the trigger guard with just one finger. She rested the weapon on the stone floor and shoved it toward Paulos with her boot.

The monk bent over, never taking his eyes or his aim from his target. He stood up with a gun in each hand - one on April and the other on Lincoln.

"Yes," he said coldly. "I know where the staircase is. But I will not allow you to go there."

"You bastard," April said with venom. "You have it, don't you? You lied to us."

"As you did to me," he said. "You are no woman of the cloth. And you are no priest."

Lincoln held his hands up. "Okay, that is true. But we had to do it for your protection. The Prince would have come in shooting if we didn't hide ourselves."

"My protection?" Paulos shook his head. "We are quite well protected, my deceitful friend."

"Who's deceitful?" April spat.

"What about the Prince?" Lincoln asked. "He is also well-protected."

"That is the case, is it? I can see only one course of action."

"You want our help?" April said. "Give us our guns and we'll help."

Paulos turned an eye to April. "You are in the exact position you need to be in to assist in ridding this monastery of our nuisance Prince."

Lincoln hesitated to ask what that meant, exactly.

Paulos continued, "You will walk through that door and back toward the helicopter. There you will remain with me. Argus will send the Prince out so we can make an offering."

Lincoln narrowed his eyes. "Offering?"

"We want you gone from this place, and the Prince, as well. I offer you to him, along with the Fallen Star. That is the relic which you seek, is it not?"

April swore under her breath.

"I give the Prince the Fallen Star, and together you leave. What he does with you is his business. I am only interested in it happening away from here."

"You wouldn't," Lincoln said in challenge. "Why would you give it to him?"

For the first time, Paulos cracked what could be considered a slight grin. "Do you truly believe you are the first people to come here looking for the Fallen Star? Do you not trust that we have methods for dealing with these people? My friend, the Prince needs not the Fallen Star, but only the idea that what he carries is indeed the object which he seeks."

April almost laughed out loud. "You're a real piece of work, Paulos."

"Why would you hide it?" Lincoln asked. "It could help a lot of people. Why don't you use it for good?"

"Men like you seek it out even when its existence remains secret," Paulos said. "Men like the Prince come here with armed troops looking to take it by force, by any means necessary. More will come, as they have come before you. How many do you believe will come once it is known to the world? What lengths do you suppose entire nations would go to extract it from our secluded domain? What wars will begin? In the quest to wield the power to save lives, how many lives do you expect will be taken?"

Paulos shook his head. It sounded to Lincoln as if he had given this speech many times before.

"No one can wield that power," Paulos continued. "It will be taken from them, as you attempt to take it for yourselves. It must remain here, in secret."

"And what do you think the Prince will do once he finds out you gave him a phony?" April asked. "He'll come back."

"As I have said, we have methods of dealing with individuals like him."

Lincoln drew a breath. The only hope was Simone, trapped down in the dark. He had to find a way to warn her, let her know they were coming, that she could no longer trust anyone.

But how?

* * *

Solomon watched from the peak where the helicopter dropped him off. Prince Kamal never asked why he wanted to be let off a quarter of a mile away from the monastery.

He knelt on the hard ground and opened the large rectangular case given to him by Murad Abdullah.

Inside was a state-of-the-art sniper rifle.

Solomon assembled the beast of a weapon with a smile. He knew that as soon as Simone Winifred Cassidy poked her unfortunate head out of the monastery, she would be dead before she ever heard the shot.

Through the scope, Solomon had a clear view of the steps leading up to the top of the rock formation. There was nowhere to hide, no cover on the initial way down. She'd be exposed, unaware, and soon - dead. His only hope was that Prince Kamal didn't get to her first.

No, she's resilient, he reminded himself. *Resilient and smart.*

That's what made her such an intriguing target. He felt like a hunter looking to claim a trophy kill. It wouldn't be easy, but the satisfaction of personally taking down the woman responsible for Heather Severn's death and the dissolution of SWANN would be a prize no trophy could match.

He watched the courtyard where the helicopter was parked, its blades still. Nobody had come out of the building since Prince Kamal went inside.

But they would. And Solomon would be ready.

From the corner of his eye, he spotted a vehicle approaching on the ground in the valley far below. The dirt it kicked up with its fast approach made it easy to see. Stealth was not a priority for whoever it was driving quickly toward the base of the rock formation on which the monastery stood.

Curious, Solomon turned away from the scope to watch.

As the vehicle drew nearer, he thought it looked like a panel van but was too far away to be certain.

It parked close to the base of the rock formation. Two men got out. They were dressed the same as Prince Kamal's bodyguards.

Curiosity turning to intrigue, Solomon turned the sniper rifle toward the van to look through the scope.

The closer view proved his suspicions correct. A van hauling some kind of equipment, but the angle it was parked at made it impossible for Solomon to get a clearer view of the inside.

He suddenly remembered the two men Prince Kamal had sent down the stairs. Panning the sniper rifle, eye to the scope, he found them approaching the parked van.

"What do you have going on, Prince?" he asked himself.

Three of the four men unloaded the van while the other inspected the base of the rock itself. Then he did something strange.

He began marking the rock.

Drawing small circles, the man moved around the base, adding another circle to the rock every few dozen paces.

As the van was emptied and the equipment assembled, Solomon's intrigue turned to puzzlement.

He watched the four men work, checking the monastery up above for signs of activity, but all was quiet outside.

What was happening below became evident when the crate of explosive charges was opened.

The four men broke into teams of two, each working their own machines.

Drilling machines.

They wasted no time. Both drills were positioned and engaged, boring into the base of the rock formation.

"Prince, you crazy bastard."

He didn't just want to steal the Fallen Star. He wanted to make a statement in doing so.

He was going to bring down the monastery.

22.

Thessaly, Greece

"Dammit!"

Simone let the lighter go out as the flame burned her thumb once more.

She put her thumb in her mouth and thought. Lincoln had said he was on his way down, but he should have been here already. He was taking too long.

Something was wrong. Simone knew it in her heart, but she didn't know what had happened. She just knew she was alone, on her own with nobody coming to help.

She had to find a way to the Fallen Star, but without a flashlight, the task seemed insurmountable.

"Cursed," she said to herself, reminded of her time in Mexico.

She shivered in the cold darkness and flicked the lighter once more.

The feeble little flame did its best to guide her way, but she couldn't make it far before needing to rest her thumb.

Eventually, after a series of lighter flicks, progress, and pauses in the dark, Simone came to a bend in the path.

Turning the corner, she saw something that brought her hope.

Torches.

Burnt out and ancient, they lined the walls on either side. She pulled one from the sconce where it hung and brought the lighter's flame to the old wood.

It smoked and sizzled, but did not light.

"Crap. Okay, Simone. Time to think."

She needed a stronger flame. Maybe a strip of clothing, like what Lincoln had used in the Aztec cave?

No, that would burn out too quickly. She needed something better, a more substantial fuel source.

A lightbulb flickered in her head.

Simone took the small bottle of whiskey from her pocket and flicked the lighter to read the label.

100 proof. It just might work.

She felt a rush as excitement as she set the torch down in the dark. Crouching there, Simone held the lighter in the firm grip of one hand while she worked the bottle open. She couldn't risk setting the lighter down and losing it in the dark, or fumbling with trying to get it in and out of her pocket.

When the bottle was open, she pawed for the torch that she held on the ground between her feet. Simone felt for the end and brought the open bottle to the old wood, letting the contents spill onto the torch.

She counted three seconds and stopped. Not enough alcohol and it would not light the wood. It had to be just the right amount.

Simone set the bottle down between her feet and stood, wiping the whiskey from her hand before handling the lighter.

Holding her breath and praying that her plan would work, Simone flicked the lighter and brought it to the end of the torch.

The pitch-black passageway lit up in a flash as the alcohol burned brightly before shrinking to a small flame, dwindling on the edge of existence.

She needed something more. It wasn't enough.

Thinking fast, Simone tore one sleeve from her t-shirt and wrapped it around the extinguishing end of the torch. She dumped a bit more whiskey and the cloth caught fire.

She held out the torch, watching the flame grow and hold steady.

It wouldn't last forever. She had to keep moving.

Simone continued onward, through the passage that had been carved directly into the rock. She had to crouch at times to avoid bumping her head.

The path curved again, in the same direction as before. She felt the decline.

She was descending deeper into the rock.

It seemed as good a place as any to hide an object of value. She wondered how many people had descended into the passage over the last hundred years. It couldn't be more than a handful.

The strange yet familiar feeling of trespassing crept over her as she continued on the downward slope. It was the same feeling from the ossuary in Brno. The feeling that she didn't belong there, that she should turn around and go back, even though what she was looking for was almost within reach.

Stealing again, she thought. *Is that why we're here?*

She wondered what she would do with the Fallen Star once she found it. Take it back to Clark? What would he do with it? The same thing he did with the Serpent's Fang?

Simone shoved the thought away. The torchlight dwindled, fading the passageway to black. She poured a little more whiskey and re-lit the torch.

Before tucking away the bottle, she allowed herself a sip. Just a small one. She might need the rest to get back up to the top. But she also needed a little stress reliever. With no painkillers on hand, she had to use what was available.

The 100 proof whiskey burned going down, but it burned so good. She could have used a second sip, but told herself that she was strong enough to save it.

Simone halted just then as the passageway opened up into a larger, rectangular room that stretched out before her.

On either side of the room, there stood stone pedestals with gold plates resting on top. She stepped forward for a closer look.

Leaning into the plate, Simone saw there was a liquid inside, thick and rank, almost like oil.

Curious now, Simone lowered the torch to the plate. The contents went up in an instant blaze. Simone jumped back, jerking the torch away.

It was like an oil lamp, she considered. Maybe the monks would carry a lantern or something down the winding ramp and light these lamps in order to see.

She strode over to the other lamp and used the torch to light it.

The room now glowed in tones of hot amber.

As the torch went out in Simone's hand, she lowered the end into the burning oil and carefully pulled it away, now wielding a much stronger flame than before.

She found a sconce on the wall. Swapping the unlit torch for the one in her hand, she brought the new torch to the flame and now had two lit torches - the one on the wall and the one in her hand.

With a renewed vigor, she felt as if she could do anything.

Simone pressed onward, toward the end of the room and through an arched doorway.

Her feet suddenly stopped, freezing her in place as a thought sprang to the front of her mind. A grim thought. A thought of the Aztec cave.

She hadn't yet encountered any booby traps, but that didn't mean there weren't any up ahead. She had been lulled into a false sense of security. If a trap did exist down in the rock, it would likely be nearby.

With extreme caution, Simone continued forward, albeit at half her previous speed, taking the time to examine her surroundings down to the finer details.

The walkie-talkie at her hip jarred her from her self-imposed trance.

It wasn't Lincoln's voice, and it wasn't April's, either. It sounded like general noise rather than a conversation.

Maybe he bumped the switch by accident?

No, because the sound continued.

Simone listened carefully, bringing the device closer to her ear. She heard voices but couldn't place who they belonged to. Their words sounded firm and direct, not conversational whatsoever.

She thought she heard Lincoln say something. Yes, he said "Okay."

The whistle of wind sounded and Simone imagined that Lincoln had stepped outside onto the courtyard. Other voices mingled in, and one of them commanded someone to "Stand over there. Don't move."

April asked, "Then what?"

"Shut up," someone told her.

"Oh, crap," Simone said out loud. Something was wrong up top. Very wrong.

She clipped the walkie to her belt and continued with her heart weighing heavily in her chest.

At length, she came to a staircase cut into the rock, steep and haphazard. The edges of the steps had been rounded smooth in the center by ages of use.

The figure she had in her head, she realized, of travelers descending into the dark caverns below the monastery was much higher than her original estimate. These steps had been used far more than she ever expected.

A chill hung in the air as she climbed deeper and deeper into the rock below the monastery. She figured she had to be close to the bottom, or at least more than half-way down.

She was idly wondering why the place on the scroll had been referred to as the Tomb of Souls when she paused, holding her breath and listening.

A grinding, rumbling sound came from below.

It was faint and distant, but present. It wasn't her imagination. The sound halted momentarily, then resumed. She could feel the rock below her feet vibrating as the noise picked up again.

"Okay, what the hell is *that?*"

She eased back into a slow pace down the steps, emerging into another rectangular room with the same oil lamps near both side walls.

Simone lit each lamp, revealing a sight every bit as macabre as the Czech ossuary.

Bones.

Thousands of them.

Stacked neatly on wooden shelves along the walls. Dozens of shelves with countless bones. The skulls had been lined up to face the center of the room. The firelight danced over their frozen expressions, leaving the hollow black sockets of dead eyes vacant and lifeless.

Simone found herself in the middle of it all, drifting in a circle and taking in the horrors of the burial crypt with her mouth agape.

She no longer wondered why the chamber was referred to as the Tomb of Souls.

"They are the bones of prior monks," a haunting voice echoed.

Simone's heart skipped a beat. She hadn't seen or heard anyone approaching.

From the shadows, a form appeared. Black robes swept the floor as he approached, melting into the orange glow of the oil lamps to reveal a gun pointed at Simone's heart.

Her body moved quicker than her mind. Before she knew it, she was diving behind the nearest stone pedestal on which the flickering lamps rested, behind the only cover she could find.

A shot rang out in the cold stone chamber.

A spray of fine stones rained past Simone as the bullet hit the rock she dove for. Her torch gone from her grasp in the desperate dive, she crouched behind the rock with nothing to defend herself.

"We've guarded this place for many, many years," the voice called. It was a voice she recognized.

Demetrius.

"And we continue to guard it. The dead and the living, we monks guard this tomb."

Simone heard the shuffle of his feet against the filthy stone floor. He was getting closer.

Think, Simone. Think!

"If it is any solace," Demetrius said, "you will not be the first to perish here."

Her breath caught in her throat, Simone had an idea and she knew she had to act. It was a crazy idea, but it had to be done.

Before the gun-wielding monk could get another word in, Simone jumped up, her hands going to the plate of fire. She didn't think twice. Hands burning, she flipped the flaming plate of oil toward the advancing monk.

Simone cried out and rolled out of the way, sprinting for the torch she had dropped, the flame still bright and strong. She grabbed for it with hands that smelled of burning flesh.

The oil struck Demetrius like a bath of fire, setting his robes ablaze.

Screaming and thrashing like mad, the monk filled the rocky cavern with the terrifying wails of a dying man.

Simone didn't mean to burn him alive, but he came up so fast. She just meant to cut off his path to her.

Grabbing the torch, Simone saw the entrance to the next chamber. She ran for it as much as she ran from the horrifying cries, the inhuman sounds of the monk who could not escape his flaming robes.

Coughing on the stench of burning human flesh, Simone came through to the next chamber gagging, unable to breathe properly.

When she was finally able to collect herself, she wiped her eyes and then had to wipe them again to make sure she wasn't seeing things.

A stone altar stood at the center of the square room, illuminated by a shaft of daylight. It made no sense, but she approached with caution, fixated on the glowing object atop the altar.

There it rested in the shaft of light, beckoning her, radiating an aura of something Simone had never seen or heard of. It was a stone, polished to a brilliant sheen and cut like a jewel. It was the size of her fist, and there wasn't a spot on it. It spoke of purity.

The Fallen Star.

Simone gazed deeply into the crystalline antiquity. For the moment, she forgot all else that was happening, but the silence that filled the room startled her all of a sudden.

The grinding rumble in the rock below. It was gone.

The altar room was still. The only sound was the crackling of her torch burning.

She scratched the side of her face, pondering what to do. If she lifted the Fallen Star, what would happen next?

Her thoughts went to Lincoln and April above. They needed her help. She couldn't waste any more time.

Simone took one last swig of the whiskey and returned the bottle to her pocket. She calculated how quickly she could run back to the doorway and get to the stairs if the artifact was at all booby-trapped.

"Okay, let's do this."

She sucked a deep breath and reached for the Fallen Star.

Lifting it in her hand, she was struck by how light it felt. Far lighter than she ever imagined. It weighed almost nothing.

Turning, Simone went for the door.

She stepped closer and closer, one foot at a time until she reached the door and nothing happened.

Looking back to the shaft of light, she gazed upon the empty altar before turning to leave.

In the next room, Simone averted her eyes to avoid the burning corpse of Demetrius.

Only, Demetrius was no longer there.

Her blood ran cold. Sweat beaded on her forehead.

Simone heard the shot without seeing where it came from.

The bullet whizzed by her face, coming within an inch of one of her braids.

Simone ducked, carrying the torch and the Fallen Star, and dove for cover behind the nearest stone pedestal.

"My people have been here for many years protecting the Fallen Star," Demetrius wailed from the darkness. "You shall not leave here with it!"

Adrenaline pumping, Simone sucked heavy breaths. She shoved the Fallen Star into one of her cargo pants pockets, thinking quickly about how to get out.

Leaning up and over with the torch, she lit the lamp above, igniting the plate of oil. If she had to throw this one, too, she would do what had to be done.

Another gunshot rang deafeningly loud, the bullet pinging against the stone pedestal in front of Simone.

She tossed a glance to the steps. She had to cross nearly the entire room. She was quick, but not as quick as a bullet.

Another shot burst through the cold air. Simone couldn't tell how close Demetrius was. Her ears rang. Her hands ached from the burns. Her mind raced.

She felt the final seconds of her life closing in, the same feeling she had just before drowning. A certainty pressing down. An ache grew in her chest.

But this time, she didn't panic. She knew what she had to do.

Simone jumped out from behind the stone pedestal, torch in hand. Her eyes searching the dim light, she saw his shadowed form.

With a flick of her wrist and her feet still on the move, Simone flung the torch at Demetrius.

Javelin and shot put were less concerned about accuracy than distance, but she was always skilled in each event.

The flaming torch cartwheeled through the air, whistling straight for the burned monk.

She heard the strike but didn't look. Her eyes remained locked on the stairs ahead, just beyond the archway.

Sucking cold air, her lungs burned. She pushed herself hard, past the point of comfort, through a barrier she didn't know was holding her back.

Listening through ringing ears as she ran, Simone waited for the gunshot she knew was coming. It wasn't a matter of if, but when.

She closed the distance to the archway faster than she thought possible. She ran too fast to stop, and collided with the rock wall on the other side of the archway.

Turning for the stairs, Simone bounded upward, making it three steps before she heard the sound.

It wasn't a gunshot. It was something worse. Much worse.

The ground beneath her feet surged upward in a sudden and violent upheaval, shattering the walls and floor of solid rock into pieces. Sent tumbling, she lost all sense of direction. Storms of boulders and stone collided in the loudest cacophony she had ever heard.

She cried out, pummeled by the stairs breaking upward, the walls rending asunder, and then she was falling. Slamming her eyes shut and covering her head, Simone screamed for help as the rock-cut cavern buckled upward in an explosive thrust and collapsed into itself, the colossal chunks of wall and floor settling in a haphazard heap and burying her in an avalanche of stone.

23.

Thessaly, Greece

Solomon raised his eye from the scope at the thunder of the explosion.

The drill team was blown away by the blast. Their van burst into flames and the remainder of the explosives went up in a cataclysmic cloud of fire.

"Hoooooooly shit…"

Solomon's jaw dropped. That wasn't supposed to happen. The team would have evacuated, but the first set of explosives planted into the rock base had detonated without warning, and now none of the four men in the valley below were left alive to finish the task.

Solomon watched the base of the rock crumple as mounds of rock were hurled in a cloud of dust.

He snapped back to the top where the helicopter was waiting. Everyone that had gathered in the courtyard had fallen as the monstrous pillar of stone became unstable. A critical fissure opened from the base, reaching to the very top, splitting the gathering of foes from the chopper with a large gash in the stone floor.

The end with the chopper sank with a brutal grunt as unstable rocks settled down below. The pilot scrambled to get into the cockpit seat. He had the blades spinning in record time.

Solomon brought his eye back to the scope. He saw Prince Orimer Kamal shouting at the pilot, his bodyguards pulling captives April and Lincoln to their feet.

A tremor shook the courtyard.

A minute later, the helicopter took off. The slab of rock on which it had been parked gave way, free-falling over the cliff and crashing into the valley with a tremendous impact.

Another minute went by before the aftershock tremors ceased and the dust began to settle.

Solomon scanned the courtyard through the scope. He accounted for everyone except two monks, one of the Prince's bodyguards, and Simone.

Panning the rifle, he searched among the windows of the various interconnected buildings but there was no movement inside. No signs of life.

"Don't tell me…"

He exhaled slowly, wondering if she would ever make it out of the monastery.

Half of the courtyard sloped toward the edge as the rock below had sunk from the explosion. A sheer drop off the side would await anyone who slipped on that slope and fell.

The helicopter hovered overhead. Solomon watched the pilot gesticulate wildly toward the Prince, adamant about not landing there again. The Prince threw his arms in the direction of the steps.

Solomon moved the rifle to see that the steps had been wrecked from the splintering of the rock. Any attempt to use them would likely be a fatal mistake.

He turned away from the scope and peered down to the source of the explosion.

The base of the rock formation had been significantly damaged, but at that moment appeared stable.

Bringing his eye back to the scope, Solomon cracked a smile.

If Simone was still alive, there was nowhere for her to go.

* * *

Lincoln scanned the courtyard but could not locate the guns he and April had been forced to drop.

Prince Kamal had made them place their weapons on the ground at their feet and kick them away, but the explosion from below had taken care of distancing Lincoln and April from the firearms. Now the guns were gone, likely thrown over the sloping, destroyed cliff that was once part of the courtyard.

All Lincoln could think of was whether or not Simone was okay. She was down there, somewhere below, underneath the monastery. She was closer to the source of the blast than anyone up top.

He had to get to her. The Fallen Star did not even enter into his mind. For all he knew, it was lost forever, buried under a hundred tons of blown-up stone.

The more he thought about it, the less likely it seemed that Simone was still living. She'd already faced clinical death once on this expedition. He'd brought her back once, but he felt a crushing doubt that he would be able to do anything else for her.

He watched as Prince Kamal screamed and waved his arms wildly at the helicopter pilot, who circled the vehicle around the monastery. There was nowhere safe to land, but it seemed that the Prince did not care. He wanted a way off the top of the rock and that was that.

The pilot shook his head, refusing to land. The Prince called out, something about a ladder or rope to pull himself up, but the pilot's head did not stop shaking.

It appeared that the Prince, along with everyone else in the courtyard, was stranded.

Almost as if reading his thoughts, April tapped Lincoln on the arm covertly, so as not to draw attention to their conversation.

"There's a way off," April said in a low voice.

Lincoln's eyes asked where.

April nodded toward the other end of the monastery. "There's a little cable car running to the plateau behind us."

"How do you know that?"

"Saw it on the tour," she said. "We have to get to it before one of our monk friends informs the Prince."

"Simone is still down there. We can't leave without her."

"Okay," April said. "But we'll need guns. We're toast if a firefight breaks out. There's nowhere to run once we're on the cable car."

Lincoln spotted the helicopter circling back around, closing in on the monastery. The Prince's attention still hung on the incoming chopper.

"I have one in my bag," April said. "Back in the room."

Lincoln gave a short nod. "Get it. I'll get to Simone. We'll rendezvous at the cable car."

"Works for me."

Lincoln held his gaze on the chopper hovering near the edge of the broken area of the courtyard, as if attempting to get as close as he could.

"When do we make a break for it?" he said in a louder voice so April could hear.

"Now," she said.

With all eyes in the courtyard dawn to the helicopter, April and Lincoln darted back into the monastery.

"Hey!"

One of the bodyguards spotted their retreat, but Prince Kamal failed to hear the cry of alarm over the thunderous chopper blades spinning so close.

"HEY!"

The Prince then turned, a mask of pure hatred burning into his features.

Lincoln sprinted down the hall with April before she peeled off into her quarters.

"Good luck," Lincoln said as he ran.

He didn't stop to see if April had found her gun or not. He kept moving, eyes searching for anything resembling a staircase.

Several of the stone walls of the monastery had cracked, and areas of the floor buckled from the displacement below.

Through one of the larger cracks in the wall, Lincoln spotted a darkness plunging down into the floor.

He almost ran right by it. The staircase had been tucked away, purposefully difficult to notice.

Without hesitating, Lincoln raced down the stairs. His hand went into his pocket and came out with a flashlight. Flicking it on, he watched the steps carefully, darting side to side to avoid broken and missing areas on the steps.

He leaped over the last half-dozen steps and found himself in a cold, dark tunnel below the main structure of the monastery.

"Simone!" he called out, but only his own voice echoed back.

He called her name again and again, checking every corner of every area he could find, but there was no sign of her.

Some rooms had caved in on themselves, others were missing their floor. He ran the flashlight over everything, making sure she wasn't trapped beneath the piles of blown-out walls and ceilings.

"Simone!"

She did not answer.

Lincoln hurried now, his heart galloping in his chest as the possibility of finding her crushed to death grew with each passing second.

He jerked to a sudden halt at the sound. Something between a tap and a thud, over and over again, drawing nearer.

It wasn't Simone.

It was the Prince's bodyguards bounding down the stairs.

24.

Thessaly, Greece

Simone opened her eyes in the dark, gagging on the plume of dust that hung in the air.

Faint light flickered from somewhere below. Or was it to the side? She didn't even know which direction was up.

She cried out in pain as she tried to move her left arm, finding it trapped beneath a massive stone. She didn't think the arm was broken. She could still wiggle her fingers, but that was all she could do with it immobilized beneath the boulder.

Simone moved her leg, wincing in pain as she felt glass from the shattered whiskey bottle digging deep into her thigh. The wound burned as the 100 proof alcohol seeped in. Clamping her teeth together and grunting through the agony, Simone managed to get herself onto her knees. She didn't have much room to work with inside the pocket of rubble. The rock below her was jagged, cutting into her knees as she knelt.

Finding a better position for her feet and bracing herself for leverage, Simone tucked her right hand under the massive stone that pinned her arm, and pulled upward with all of her strength.

It wouldn't budge.

Huffing and sweating, hair plastered to her dirty face, Simone tried again but she knew it wouldn't move. At least not upward. There was too much pressure from above.

She tried a different approach, shifting her legs around and planting both boots on the stone with her back to, she guessed, the wall.

"Okay, you can do this…"

Freeing her arm could cause the rocks piled above to collapse down on her, but it was a risk she had to take. She couldn't get out without first freeing her trapped arm.

Hesitating from a mixture of fear and the pain of the alcohol-soaked wound in her leg, Simone pulled the broken bottle fragments out and let them fall between the rocks. She heard the pieces *tink-tinkling* all the way down until she couldn't hear them anymore.

She took a huge breath. "Okay. Okay, okay, okay … you can do this."

With her heart beating in her throat, Simone pressed both of her boots to the rock once more, knees up against her face, and shoved with all of the strength in her legs.

Crying from the pressure on her arm, Simone didn't stop. She kept shoving, knowing her legs were the strongest part of her body and the only chance she had at moving the massive stone.

With a final burst of effort, Simone felt the pressure on her arm disappear. The massive stone slipped away, crashing below.

Small rocks pebbled down where the stone once sat, but nothing major had fallen in its place. Nothing collapsed onto her. She was free and, for the moment, still alive.

Simone took a moment to sit back, arm pulled into her chest as she caught her breath and let herself calm down.

She'd thought she was dead again. She had thought her life was permanently over as the world was thrown into immediate chaos. Her body ached from countless bruises and contusions. Her arm throbbed. Her leg burned. Her hands felt numb. Her thoughts were in a fog. Only then did she realize that she'd lost some time between the implosion and her waking up in a cocoon of jagged stone.

She felt the back of her head and her hand came away bloody. She wondered what else had happened to her that she didn't know about yet.

Pushing herself up to her knees once again, Simone knew she had to keep moving before the adrenaline wore off. She'd be useless once the effects of injury caught up. She had to get out of the cave before then.

Cursed, she thought. *I've gotta be cursed.*

She didn't want to entertain the idea, but it was the only thing that made sense. Everywhere she went, disaster struck. People were hurt or killed, including herself.

Before she began the search for an exit, Simone felt in her pocket for the Fallen Star.

Miraculously, she still had it.

Digging it out of her pocket, Simone held the glimmering jewel between both hands, wincing from the pain in her arm, not so sure about it being unbroken anymore.

But she held a healing object, and with the little bit of resolve the thought gave her, Simone closed her eyes and waited for the effects to take place.

A minute later, she opened her eyes, tears dripping from her eyelashes.

Nothing had happened.

Her hands were still burned. The pain in her arm grew more severe. Her leg still ached.

"What the…"

She assumed the Fallen Star wouldn't come with an instruction manual, but it should be straightforward. It was known to heal, yet it did nothing to her, the effect nonexistent.

Simone wiped her face with her good hand, wondering if she was doing all this for nothing, getting herself drowned and blown up and her body broken, all for a shiny rock that wasn't special at all.

What she needed was another bottle of painkillers, not some mythical object that might or might not be a total hoax.

With a huff of determination, Simone tucked the Fallen Star back into her pocket. She knew she had to move.

As she maneuvered over haphazard piles of the shattered walls and stairs, Simone found it harder and harder to see. It was good that she was making her way upward, throwing herself over mounds of rock and slinking through tunnels when any other option was found to be impossible, but she was moving farther and farther away from the firelight below.

She still had the lighter in her pocket. Every so often, she pulled it out and flicked it on, moving it over the stones and along the walls to see where she could fit her body next. There wasn't any way of knowing if she was going the right way, but it was the only way, so it had to be right.

Otherwise, she was trapped.

It was slow going with her left arm compromised. It was badly bruised and swollen, and the dexterity in her hand and fingers was half of what it was normally. She clambered over the piles of rock mostly with her legs and one arm, doing her best to get out as soon as possible in case another incident occurred.

What even happened?

The only thing she could guess was an earthquake. She considered the region - Greece - and then recalled three of the Seven Wonders of the Ancient World that had been built near Greece had been destroyed by earthquakes.

With every new step and every effort to pull herself up, the possibility of further collapse weighed heavily on Simone's mind. Yet she climbed on, determined to free herself from the Tomb of Souls.

She paused more often than she would have liked, but she still wasn't herself after what had happened in Dubai. A weakness clung to her, refusing to allow her to keep pressing on as she normally would. Her limits had been reconfigured, and it frustrated her to the point of anger.

Crawling through a tunnel of rock, Simone emerged on the other side and came into a more open area, one nearly untouched by the effects of the blast.

She sat with her back to the wall, left arm held against her stomach and right hand clutching the glass wound in her leg, which bled through her fingers.

It took a full minute for her to catch her breath. She counted every second, and with every second her disappointment with herself grew.

She knew she was better than this. She knew she could stand up and keep going. She knew this mentally, but her body told a different story. She was drained, exhausted, desperate for rest. She knew she hadn't yet reached her limit, but she felt that way nonetheless.

Simone cursed out loud, and forced herself up to her feet. She was going to keep going until she dropped, unable to move another inch. That would be the only thing to stop her.

Before long, Simone found herself in familiar territory. The large gallery room with torches on the walls.

The room was absolutely black and only the flicking of her lighter gave any indication as to where she was. But through the dim glow of the tiny flame, the room appeared unaffected by the cataclysmic event.

Simone found a torch on the wall, ripped off the other sleeve of her t-shirt, and wrapped it around the business end of the torch.

She worked the lighter's flame against the dirtied fabric. The whiskey was gone, so she had to hope that the tiny lighter flame would be strong enough to eat through the grime she'd picked up on the shirt sleeve.

When the cotton began burning, she almost jumped for joy, only her leg was aching from the glass and her feet felt numb from the punishment of scaling broken rocks.

Torch in hand, Simone continued on with an even stronger determination. Maybe it was all in her head, but she felt rejuvenated, less tired, and more than ever, ready to get herself out of the hole under the monastery.

She hurried on, the new swell of resolve kicking her into a higher gear. Along the way as she passed through the dark, her torch lighting the way, lost in her thoughts, Simone almost didn't hear the voice ahead, calling to her from around several corners.

She stopped, lowering the torch so the crackling of flames eating away at the old wood wasn't so close to her still-ringing ears.

"*Simone!*"

It was Lincoln's voice, calling her name.

"Lincoln!" she shouted, and pressed on, pushing herself into a painful sprint.

Simone came swiftly to the heavy stone door that had masked the mouth of the hallway - her original entrance into the dark unknown. Into the Tomb of Souls.

"Simone, hurry!"

Lincoln stood beyond the stone door, facing a gap much narrower than Simone remembered.

Her eyes fell to the large boulder she had rolled into place to prop the door open, and her heart sank when she saw that it had been cracked, either from the constant pressure or from the massive tremor below, or both.

The stone door itself appeared canted, angled down-ward, shifted from its track due to the violent force of the explosion.

"Crap," she said as the dread of being trapped where she was crept in.

The gap had already been narrow, but now she could-n't even fit her head through the small space.

Lincoln reached an arm in for Simone to take. "We've gotta move, now!"

But Simone stood her ground, knowing the effort would be futile. Even a child would have a hard time slipping through the gap.

Without debate, Simone took the Fallen Star from her cargo pants pocket and put it in Lincoln's hand.

"Take it," she said. "I'll find another way out."

"Simone, wait!"

Lincoln pulled the ancient artifact through. His hand returned open.

"Take my hand," he said. "There's no time!"

Simone stepped back, her decision made. "I'll find another way. Go!"

She hurried away from the door, back in the direction she had just come, not waiting for a reply, not permitting any more discussion.

There had to be another way out.

There just *had* to be.

25.

Thessaly, Greece

"God *dammit*, Simone!"

He both hated and loved that she was so stubborn. What if there was no other way out? What if the cavern collapsed?

But she was right, Lincoln knew. He had to get himself out, and get the Fallen Star to back to Clark.

He gazed upon the artifact in his hands. It appeared to glow dimly in the blackness of the tunnel. It looked to be a polished stone, angular and beautiful, but like nothing he had ever seen.

Holding it tight, Lincoln raced through the tunnel's winding corridors, avoiding the sounds of Prince Kamal's men fast approaching.

He didn't realize how maze-like the area below the monastery truly was. He was getting himself lost, but hiding was the only way to protect himself and the Fallen Star without a gun in his hand.

Using the flashlight as sparingly as possible, Lincoln ran as silently as he could, nimble-footed around corners and down the long stretches of hallway.

He checked a storage area to his left, glimpsing the familiar sight of boxes of hops stacked against one wall. It was a beer-making supply room, and he'd passed it on his way down.

Oriented now, Lincoln turned another corner and found himself face to face with the broken staircase he had used to descend.

He tucked the Fallen Star into his pocket and climbed.

At the top of the steps, he poked his head out, glancing down both ends of the hall. Nobody was around.

Success. All he had to do was turn right and follow the layout of the buildings to the end where April would be waiting.

Lincoln turned right and vanished down the hall.

He didn't know which way to go from there, so he hooked a right and then a quick left, continuing on in the general direction of the cable car that would deliver him to safety.

The hallway ended and curved left. Lincoln rounded the bend and his boots ground to a dead stop beneath him.

Argus held a gun to Lincoln's face. "Going somewhere?"

Lincoln's hands went up instinctively, showing he wasn't a threat.

"Turn around," Argus commanded. "The Prince is waiting for you."

Lincoln did as he was told, walking back in the direction he had come.

"What are you doing, Argus?" he asked. "You don't have to deal with him. Let us go and let him find his own way home."

"My friend, you fail to understand, as does Brother Paulos. There is a fortune to be made. Fate has smiled down upon us this day."

"I hate to remind you," Lincoln said as he walked, "but the whole place is about to collapse."

"I am well aware, and if not for you and your friends, the Fallen Star might have been lost beneath the rubble."

Argus stopped walking, pointing the gun in the direction of Lincoln's pocket.

"But that is not the case, is it?" Argus asked.

Lincoln turned to face the monk. "Are you really going to give it away? To Prince Kamal, of all people? Argus, listen…"

"I have listened to it all before. Reasoning. Begging. Pleading. In this very hallway, I have heard it. Many have come in search of the Fallen Star, but you shall be the last. Hand it to me."

The monk held out his free hand.

Lincoln exhaled. He felt his chances of success slipping away with his very breath, and his chances of making it off of the rock dwindled down to nothing.

Reluctant but left with no other choice, Lincoln handed the Fallen Star to Argus.

The monk smiled a wicked grin. "Keep moving."

Lincoln turned and continued on, step by step to his fate.

He felt like a prisoner walking to his own execution.

* * *

Simone thought she caught a glimpse of sunlight peeking through the rocks above.

Climbing over a fallen section of wall, Simone scaled a mound of rubble and brought her face close to a small break between the top of a wall and the ceiling.

She couldn't get the best view, but as she craned her neck to the side and angled her head so that at least one eye could see through, she found her suspicions confirmed.

Beyond the wall before her, sunlight broke through.

There was another way out.

All she had to do was get to the other side of the wall. But as she climbed down the rubble pile and inspected her surroundings, she saw no other way around.

The only way to the other side was through the wall.

She scrambled to the top of the rubble again and found some of the stones to be loose. The mortar that held the large rocks together had grown brittle with the passing ages, and the tremor from below had jostled the wall just enough.

Simone saw no other option. She had to break through.

Bracing herself as best as she could, she tested the strength of the wall by pressing her shoulder against it.

It didn't move very much at all.

She knew she couldn't throw her shoulder into the rock or she would come out in worse shape than she was already in. She had to kick it down.

Simone raised a boot and thrust her heel against the wall.

Three chunks of stone gave way, tumbling into the sunlit room beyond.

"I hope this isn't load-bearing," she said, and kicked at the wall once more.

Nothing happened.

Simone kicked and kicked again, finally breaking off a sizable portion of the wall. It was just large enough to fit through.

She pulled herself through, fitting one arm between the rock and her body, then the other, and pulled some more.

Before she could figure out how to get her legs through, the rock below collapsed and Simone free-fell to the floor as the stones tumbled down around her.

Covering her head with her hands and pulling her legs in close, Simone held her breath until the crashing of stones fell silent.

She picked herself up, a little bruised and beaten, but no worse off than she was before.

Simone gazed up at the sunlight filtering through the broken ceiling, raising a hand to shield her emerald eyes.

* * *

Alerted by the sight of Lincoln emerging from within the complex, Solomon brought his eye to the scope and shifted his aim for a better look.

One of the monks escorted Lincoln at gunpoint.

"What the hell is going on over there?"

The helicopter still hovered, but Solomon couldn't spot the pilot inside.

Then he noticed the pilot had leaned out of his seat and stretched toward the open side door.

Prince Kamal waited at the edge of the broken courtyard, arms raised to catch whatever was about to fall his way.

A backpack fell from the chopper and the pilot regained his seat at the controls.

Solomon focused on the backpack that the Prince was now strapping on.

A parachute.

Solomon smiled in spite of himself. The Prince seemed to have taken everything into account.

Everything except Lincoln batting the monk's gun away and snatching the Fallen Star from Argus. He held the glowing rock high above his head, leaning toward the edge, threatening to drop it over the side of the small stone wall and down to the valley below.

The Fallen Star. Was that what everyone was killing themselves to find? That little rock?

Solomon watched through the rifle scope as the monk with the gun lowered his weapon.

The Prince, now strapped in, stepped toward Lincoln.

Lincoln inched closer to the edge, not kidding around about dropping the object of everyone's desire.

A lightning-fast scan of the courtyard through the sniper scope failed to spot Simone. Everyone else was in the courtyard but her.

The Prince's face turned red, his anger and impatience evident even through the rifle scope.

Lincoln did not give in.

If nobody in the courtyard was going to do it, Solomon figured it was up to him.

He aimed at Lincoln, resting his finger on the trigger. He allowed his breath to steady, his heart rate to slow.

On the next exhale, Solomon pulled the trigger.

* * *

Simone's body went numb when she heard the shot crack over the open valley.

That wasn't an ordinary handgun discharging. It cut through the helicopter's blades, deafening all other sound. It came from somewhere else, not within the monastery.

Her heart beating like mad, Simone raced through the labyrinthine hallways and passages, desperate to get to the courtyard. She leaped fallen stone blocks, pushing all thoughts of pain away from her mind, adrenaline her ally.

She broke through the door to the open courtyard, finding half of it missing, shattered and fallen into the valley below.

Lincoln lay motionless, one hand pressed to his shoulder where blood flowed freely. April scrambled to reach him, but the monk Argus was trying to stop her.

April shoved the monk aside. He slipped, tumbling away. She ducked below a short stone wall where Lincoln's body lay. Immediately she checked his vitals, applying pressure to the wound, keeping her head below the wall in case another shot rang out.

Simone turned as the helicopter banked away, chased off by the sniper fire.

Standing there at the edge of the courtyard was Prince Kamal, holding the Fallen Star in his hands. He tucked it into a pouch that hung over his shoulder and stepped on top of the stone wall overlooking the sheer vertical drop.

Simone looked to Lincoln and April at her right, then to Prince Kamal at her left.

As her eyes reached the side of the courtyard where Prince Kamal stood, she caught his feet leaving the stone wall beneath him, watched as his body fell out of view, taking the Fallen Star with him.

Simone ran to her left, toward where the Prince had leaped.

Her legs pumping, heart thudding, adrenaline taking over, Simone closed in on the wall as fast as her broken body would carry her.

An explosion of rock dust and pebbles flew out from the rock wall in front of her. She heard the shot after the bullet impacted, missing her by inches.

Without thinking twice, Simone jumped as she reached the short stone wall, clearing it to the sound of April's frantic protest...

And fell.

26.

Thessaly, Greece

Simone thought she had made the last mistake of her life until she saw the Prince's parachute open below. As his descent slowed, Simone closed in fast, free-falling straight for him.

Aiming for the parachute, Simone held her breath as she impacted the fabric at speed.

Her body bounced, sliding away, hands frantically groping for anything to hold on to as a torrent of wind assailed her.

Grasping a strap, Simone's body slipped from atop the unfurled parachute, her legs slamming into the back of Prince Kamal.

Survival instinct kicked in. She wrapped her legs around his waist, knowing she was dead the second she lost hold of Prince Kamal.

"You - you crazy bitch!" he shouted, desperate to wriggle out of the grip of Simone's legs.

The extra weight, unevenly distributed, pulled the two of them in a wild descent.

The Prince struggled to shake the pesky adventurer away, but Simone's legs were too strong from years of Olympic-level training.

He swatted at her, hands balled into fists. Some punches caught air, others caught Simone in the face.

Desperate, she pulled herself up, using all of the strength in her legs and core, and wrapped her free arm around the Prince's throat. Letting go of the strap, she brought her other arm around to secure the choke hold.

He gagged for breath, but Simone had all of her upper-body weight pressing down on his carotid artery, cutting off his oxygen supply.

It wasn't long before the Prince's limbs went slack and his struggling ceased.

Holding on for dear life, Simone did her best to steer the parachute away from the cliffside and into the open valley.

The duo landed, and Prince Kamal's limp body slid across the grass, limbs splayed and unmoving.

Simone rolled onto her back, chest heaving for a calming breath. Her entire body felt numb from the rush.

Did I really just do that?

Pushing herself up, Simone slipped the Fallen Star from the Prince's pouch and held it once again.

She looked to the rocks to her left and considered what would have happened if they hadn't been so lucky in their landing. If the Fallen Star had shattered on impact, all the struggle, all the violence, all the bloodshed and death would have been for nothing.

Lincoln!

Her thoughts raced back into gear. She started for the pillar of rock on which the monastery was built, but with the steps ruined, there was no way for her to get back up.

Standing there, unconscious Prince to her right and the Fallen Star in her hand, Simone had no idea what to do next.

* * *

The helicopter took off again once Solomon was on board.

"Get me a line of sight on that courtyard!"

The pilot nodded and veered the chopper back toward the monastery.

Grinding his teeth, he cursed to himself. His shot missed. He had her lined up in the crosshairs, but the bullet went wide by no more than six inches.

Dammit!

It looked from his vantage as if Simone had jumped off the top of the monastery, but that couldn't be. She had to have ducked, or crouched, or taken cover somewhere. She had no parachute. She would be insane to jump.

Blasts of gunfire boomed below. Bullets pinged against the chopper's exterior.

"Holy shit!"

The pilot pulled away, avoiding the fire from April Farren's handgun in the courtyard below.

"What are you doing?" Solomon yelled. "Get us closer!"

"We'll be shot!"

"I don't care. Get us closer!"

The pilot shook his head adamantly. "We cannot. They will hit the fuel tank."

Exhaling sharply, Solomon let his thoughts settle. The pilot was right. They had to retreat.

"Swing around to the other side of the monastery. Make it wide if you have to, just do it."

"Then we go," the pilot said in a tone that invited no further discussion.

Solomon nodded.

The chopper made a wide arc around the monastery, remaining far out of range for any accurate handgun fire from the courtyard.

By the time the chopper came within view of the spot where the Prince had landed, Solomon saw that Prince Kamal was the only soul on the ground.

Simone had disappeared.

27.

Andrews AFB, Maryland

Simone turned her head at the sound of the door opening.

A strange feeling came over her when Clark Bannicheck walked in. It wasn't dread, fear, anger, relief, nothing. It was an alien feeling, an emotion she'd never felt before. It was a mixture of everything and nothing. She didn't know what to feel, what to say.

"Is this going to be a regular thing?" he asked. "You spending a week in the infirmary after returning?"

Simone cleared her throat. "I hope so."

Clark stepped up to the bed, chuckling. "You hope *so?*"

She nodded.

"And why is that?"

"It means I made it back alive," Simone said with half a grin.

Clark sat in the chair next to the bed. "In that respect, I, too, hope so."

Simone shifted herself in bed. She hadn't gotten much sleep. Nurses had been in and out ever since she'd returned, tending to her multitude of injuries at all hours of the night, feeding her pills and sticking her with needles. Before long, she stopped asking what was what and just let them do their thing.

She'd fractured the radius bone in her left arm, sustained a concussion, required eight staples in her head, both palms had first and second-degree burns, and she'd suffered stress fractures in both feet.

But it wasn't her wounds she was worried about.

"How's Lincoln?" she asked Clark.

"He's out of surgery and recovering well," he said. "He should be on his feet in no time."

Simone breathed a sigh of relief. From what she'd seen in a brief and fleeting glance, the shot from the sniper's rifle looked critical.

"You, on the other hand..." Clark stood. "I would really quite like it if you didn't punish yourself so much on these journeys, Miss Simone. One day, they'll be bringing you back in pieces."

"Maybe I should stay home next time," she said, only half joking.

Clark turned a curious look on her. "And why would you do that?"

Simone pressed her bandaged hands into the bed to prop herself up to a seated position.

"Tell me the truth," she said.

Clark gave a shake of his head. "I don't know what you mean..."

"I brought you the Fallen Star. I brought you the Serpent's Fang. But there's still something you're not telling me."

Clark returned to the chair beside the bed. "Is this in regard to your parents?"

Simone's hard stare said it all.

Clark lowered his eyes, sighing. "Simone-"

"Just tell me what really happened. Did they actually die in a car wreck? Was it sabotaged somehow?"

She paused, wondering if she should ask what she was about to ask.

"Did you do it?"

Clark leaned away, chuckling as if the idea was preposterous. "Miss Simone, I think we should discuss this when you're better rested."

"No," she said, the word as hard as stone. "We're discussing this now, because when I leave this bed, I'm not coming back."

Clark fixed her with a look as he failed to find the words to say, struck silent by the sudden declaration from Simone.

"You shipped me out of here as fast as you could, before I could speak to you, before I could start asking questions. But here we are now, and I've got nowhere else to be."

Clark opened his mouth to speak but Simone raised a hand, cutting him off before he got the first word out.

"You've lied to me," she continued. "You've put me in situations I wasn't prepared for or trained for. You ship me around the world like your personal assistant, and even when I come back looking like I just had a monastery dropped on my head, you don't think twice about how maybe this isn't the job for me, that I'm going to get myself killed a few more times. But that's okay, as long as you get your prize at the end?" She shook her head. "No, I'm done. I can't keep doing this, Clark. I literally cannot do it again, physically, mentally, I can't. This isn't what I do. Shootouts and snipers? I'm not a soldier. I'm…"

She struggled to find the term.

"I'm just me."

Clark watched, expressionless, not giving her any indication that she was wrong or right about anything she said.

He cleared his throat once Simone's rant was over. "You may disagree with our methods, but I assure you that everything is done the way it is for a very specific reason. That doesn't make sense to you just yet, but it will."

"When?" Simone asked without hesitation.

"Everything you're looking for is in the journal your parents kept. You do still have it, don't you?"

She nodded. "It's somewhere safe."

"Good," he said. "Because I have not made any copies. It is one-of-a-kind, and within those pages is every answer you seek."

Simone couldn't shake the feeling of confusion from her head. "It's just notes on their travels. Half of it isn't even legible. What does that have to do with anything?"

Clark raised his eyebrows and nodded in agreement. "Your father did have the worst handwriting. That's why much of it was penned by your mother. She had a way with words, you could say."

Clark stood once more.

"Keep reading, Simone. And keep it safe."

She turned him a skeptical eye. "What will I find?"

Clark started for the door. "Everything." He paused at the threshold. "And when you do, tell no one."

That was not the answer she expected to hear. She wanted to lay into him again and spill every thought and feeling she had coiled up inside, get it all off her chest and make it abundantly clear that she was making her own decisions, and that she was absolutely not coming back for another mission.

But the mystery of her parents' death tugged at her even harder.

"Wait," Simone called before he left.

Clark waited by the door.

"The Fallen Star," Simone said. "It heals, right? I could really use some of that right now."

With a chuckle, Clark said, "It's not like that."

"What's it like, then?"

"You'll see," he said. "One day, you'll see."

"Maybe I won't. Maybe I'm really not coming back."

"You will," he said with confidence. "Read the journal, then see if you feel the same."

With a short nod, Clark Bannicheck left the room.

Simone sat back, head in the clouds. She felt more confused than ever before about the Fallen Star, about why she was doing what she was doing, about the fate of her parents.

Keep it safe? What the hell does that mean?

Allowing her eyes to shut, Simone waited for the nurse to return. She wanted another dose of morphine in hopes it could lead to sleep undisturbed by the horrifying screams of the burning monk down in the Tomb of Souls.

I have to get back to Norway, she told herself.

As soon as she was well enough to walk, she was boarding the nearest flight east and returning to her apartment in Svingvoll. Wherever the journal would take her next, that's where she would go, and she wouldn't make herself so easy to find this time.

Listening to the sound of her breath, she counted down the hours until she could crack the journal open once again and dive back into the past.

The future would have to wait.

28.

Svingvoll, Norway

Solomon peered over the rim of his coffee cup, his cold stare piercing through the rising steam as he sipped.

His eyes had not left the window since he sat down inside the tiny cafe. The view of the apartment down on the corner registered to Simone Winifred Cassidy was not ideal, but it was the only place he could maintain a view of the front door without appearing overly suspicious.

He watched an older woman with blonde hair carry a box to her SUV. Solomon half-expected to see Simone herself walk out of the apartment, but it was only the landlady taking Simone's possessions away to an unknown destination.

Lilly cracked her gum while flipping pages in the journal that had once belonged to Simone's parents. She sat opposite Solomon, perfectly content to wait as long as they had to. There was plenty to read, plenty to decipher.

"There's a lot of juicy stuff in here, babe," she said without looking up.

Solomon didn't care about the travel journal, unless it could somehow tell him if and when Simone was going to return to the apartment to claim her belongings and discover that the book had vanished.

He'd sit here all day if he had to, or at least until the landlady drove off with all of Simone's worldly possessions - which wasn't very much at all.

But the journal … this was something she had to care about deeply. She wouldn't let it go for long.

It was simply a matter of time before she came looking for it.

"Did you know her parents discovered a new element?" Lilly said absently.

"Did they?" Solomon said with feigned interest.

"Yepper. Something about a meteorite - it's all scribbles. This guy's penmanship is wretched. I can write better with my ear."

Solomon grinned and sipped more of his coffee while it was still burning hot - just the way he liked it.

"They must have been at this for a while," Lilly said, flipping pages. "There's so many notes about undiscovered tombs and lost relics. Ten, fifteen, twenty. I can't even count them all. I wonder if they died before they found everything?"

"Probably," Solomon said, considering that Simone would be joining them before she found any more treasures in the wild. The Fallen Star would be her last conquest.

"So," Lilly said. "Do you think Sonja will be getting here any time soon, or should I order something else, because I'm-"

"Simone," Solomon corrected. "Her name is Simone Winifred Cassidy."

"You sure?" Lilly asked, popping a gum bubble.

"As sure as the day is long."

There was a long pause while Lilly studied the writing in the journal.

"Nah," she said. "It's definitely Sonja. Look…"She spun the book around for Solomon to read. He tore his eyes away from the window and looked to where Lilly pointed.

"Like I said, he's a scribbler, but that's definitely S-O-N-J-A."

Intrigue took over and Solomon turned to inspect the book's writings. He brought his head down for a closer look.

Lilly was right.

She shrugged. "Maybe she changed her name?"

Solomon let the question go unanswered. If Simone had once had a different name, Lilly would have found out already. She was the best at gathering information on people, looking into their past, digging up their dirt. Nobody was better.

Solomon skimmed through some more pages. The handwriting was atrocious. He couldn't make half of it out.

He slid the book toward Lilly.

She turned it back around to face her direction, her gaze lingering on Solomon's face - a face deep in thought.

"Well?" she asked. "Then who the heck is Sonja?"

* * *

Simone met with her landlady at the airport in Fagernes to retrieve her belongings. The older woman was nice enough to suggest bringing the few things to Simone rather than Simone venturing all the way into town with a cast on her left arm and both feet wrapped.

As Simone sat inside the airport waiting for her flight, her phone rang.

"Georgia, what's up?"

"Are you free to talk?" Georgia spoke in a voice so low that Simone had to concentrate to hear over the din of activity inside the terminal.

"Yeah, why? What's wrong?"

"I did some digging," Georgia whispered. "Are you safe?"

Simone checked the volume on her phone. It was already all the way up. "Are *you?* What's going on? I'm stepping on a plane any a minute."

"Are you sitting down?"

"Just talk. What did you find?"

Georgia took a heavy breath as if to prepare herself. "Your parents…"

Simone's heart leaped in her chest.

Georgia continued, "It was a car wreck."

Simone exhaled, not even realizing her breath had caught in her throat. The news was not as startling as she expected.

"I know," she said to her friend on the other end of the phone.

"But Simone … he was there."

An announcement was heard, and those sitting around Simone stood and moved to board the flight.

Simone didn't move from her seat. "Who was there?"

"On the base where it happened-"

"Georgia, *who?*"

"Clark," she said gravely. "Clark Bannicheck. He was there, Simone, on the scene when it happened. He was there. I have a photo to prove it."

The world shut out around Simone as her mind fell into a void of realization - the realization that her suspicions may have just been confirmed, that the warnings of Harald should be heeded. That Clark Bannicheck was not an ally.

A final announcement jarred Simone back to reality. She stood and limped to board the plane ready to leave Norway.

"Simone, I've gotta go," Georgia said. "We'll talk again soon. Be safe!"

"You, too."

Simone ended the call, slipped the phone back into her pocket. As she passed through the boarding bridge, she froze in place just before stepping onto the plane.

A sound echoed from outside the airport terminal, rolling between the surrounding hills, freezing Simone's blood in her veins.

It was the howl of a wolf.

Thank you for reading *The Tomb of Souls*. I hope you enjoyed this second book in the Treasure Huntress series.

The story continues in Book 3 - *Followers of the Storm*.

sunbirdbooks.org

Made in the USA
Middletown, DE
08 January 2020

82575014R00165